ROCKY MOUNTAIN BIGFOOT CAMPFIRE STORIES

ROCKY MOUNTAIN BIGFOOT CAMPFIRE STORIES

RUSTY WILSON

© 2021 Yellow Cat Publishing™ All rights reserved, including the right of reproduction in whole or in part in any form. Yellow Cat and the accompanying logo are registered trademarks owned by Yellow Cat Publishing. www.yellowcatbooks.com Any resemblance to actual persons, living or dead, or events is entirely coincidental.

For All Who Love Mystery and the Beauty of Nature

CONTENTS

Foreword   ix
Introduction   xi

1. The Winch Cat   1
2. Kintla Lake   18
3. The Burning Mountain   39
4. Terror in the Black Canyon   55
5. The Fly House   69
6. The Sawtooth Sasquatch   91
7. Stay Just A Little Bit Longer   105
8. The Most Beautiful Places   124
9. The Big Winds Blowdown   140

About the Author   153

FOREWORD

Welcome to another book of Bigfoot stories by the World's Greatest Bigfoot Storyteller, none other than Rusty Wilson!

These all new stories from all over the Rocky Mountains are sure to give you chills, yet also make you want to meet a Bigfoot—well, maybe theoretically, at least. Are you brave enough to read them at night by headlamp while camped in the deep forest? Or will you read them at home, after locking all the windows?

Fly-fishing guide Rusty Wilson has spent years collecting these tales from his clients around the campfire, stories guaranteed to make sure you won't want to go out after dark.

Come spend your night with a brave snowcat driver grooming an extreme ski slope in a most dangerous way, then join a scuba diver in Glacier National Park who meets a most unusual underwater companion. Come along as a woman discovers that her neighborhood harbors the perfect solution to cold winter nights, then experience the terror of being stalked in one of the planet's deepest and most extreme canyons.

If you survive all that, read how a newly divorced doctor finds that his idyllic rental near the Tetons has a hidden secret that comes with a flyswatter, then follow along as a lone hiker discovers the high mountains of Idaho hold more than he bargained for.

Next, help an old Wyoming rancher decide whether to sell out or stay, then visit a remote campground where rocks are the incoming thing. And finally, hike into the rugged Wind River Range of Wyoming as a strange rescue party provides a most unusual relief from hurricane-force winds.

Another great book from Rusty Wilson, Bigfoot expert and storyteller—tales for both the Bigfoot believer and those who just enjoy a good story.

INTRODUCTION

Greetings, fellow adventurers, to another collection of Bigfoot campfire stories, this group featuring one of the most beautiful, extensive, and rugged ranges in the world—the Rocky Mountains, which stretch 3,000 miles from their northernmost end in British Columbia down into New Mexico. The name of the range is supposedly from the Cree word, *assinwati,* which means, *when seen from across the prairies, they look like a rocky mass.*

The Rockies vary in width from 70 to 300 miles and have many majestic peaks, the highest being 14,440 feet Mt. Elbert in Colorado. The range has numerous subranges, including the Sangre de Cristos, the Wind River Range, the Big Horns, the Absaroka-Beartooth Ranges, the Tetons, the Wasatch, the San Juans, the Bitterroots, the Sawtooths, and many more. It's a vast region with many untouched places, in spite of how invasive we humans have become.

And better still, the numerous peaks of the Rockies protect innumerable lush mountain valleys with plentiful wildlife and plants and running water, the perfect habitat for our Bigfoot friends, who love these deep forests and backcountry, places that are still wild and free.

In actuality, pretty much all of my previous books are set in the Rockies, but I've tried to categorize them somewhat by topic or region. The stories included here are kind of what one might call a motley crew, with settings all over the Rockies instead of in just one area, so I've decided to just call it Rocky Mountain stories.

Like most of my stories, these were collected mostly from my fly-fishing clients. There's nothing like being outdoors around a fire to get folks talking, especially if you add in some mouth-watering Dutch-oven cooking. Appropriately enough, almost all were told to me along the riverways of the Rockies.

Due to habitat being more and more fragmented by human development, I believe Bigfoot is having a more difficult time following seasonally migrating game without being seen. I believe this may account for the majority of encounters and may also explain why Bigfoot is now more commonly seen than in earlier days when there were fewer people.

In any case, these stories represent only a few of the encounters people have shared with me. I've tried to include those that I find most interesting. Like I've mentioned in earlier books, I only share stories with the permission of the teller, and I always change the names of those involved and often also the places where they took place (though not always).

So, sit back with a cup of hot chocolate in a big comfy chair or by a campfire and enjoy. Get out a map and follow along, and always keep your eyes and ears open for North America's most unique and elusive creature. —Rusty

1

THE WINCH CAT

Johnny and I met while I was waiting for a friend to show up along the San Miguel River out of Placerville, Colorado, just below the famous ski town of Telluride. The San Miguel starts high in the San Juan Mountains and is one of the last untamed rivers in Colorado. My friend and I had agreed to meet for an afternoon of fishing, since I was in the area for a few days.

The San Miguel has lots of rainbow trout and what's called "cutbow," a hybrid mix of rainbow and cutthroat. We were excited to fish this stretch, and a bonus was meeting Johnny, who was also fishing. He ended up showing us a couple of good spots and then joined us for the afternoon. I enjoyed the fishing, but the most memorable part of the day was him telling me the following story. —Rusty

Rusty, I grew up in the high mountains of Colorado, the state with the highest average altitude of all 50 states. I was born and raised in Silverton, a small historic silver mining town, which is how it got its name.

Silverton sits in the caldera of an extinct volcano at an altitude of 9,318 feet and is surrounded by huge 13,000-foot mountains. There have been many times when avalanches nearly wiped out the town, so you can picture how steep the surrounding countryside is, and that was my playground growing up.

This story didn't take place there, but I mention all this so you know I was raised like a mountain goat, totally unafraid of heights. There's an extreme ski area there now with one lift, but when I was growing up, if you wanted to ski, you either travelled to nearby ski areas over one of the two high mountain passes that led out of the town, or you hiked up the steep slopes around town, an activity that was frowned on because of the avalanche danger.

There wasn't much else to do there during the long cold winters, so ski we did, though usually it was cross-country in the valley, which was safer than trying to deal with the slopes. In any case, I learned to ski pretty well, and since this was the environment I grew up in—skiing and extreme mountains—it makes sense that I would end up working at a ski area.

I left home right after high school, my little Honda piled high with my stuff, heading over Molas Pass, the southern route out of the valley over to the town of Durango, where I went to a small college. Durango is near a ski area called Purgatory Resort, and I spent every weekend there skiing instead of studying, and by the end of my first year of college, I wanted nothing more than to be a ski bum.

So, I dropped out and moved to Telluride, where there were skiing jobs. It wasn't all that far as the crow flies from Silverton—actually just over the mountain—though it took a couple of hours to get from one town to the other.

After I quit college, I spent the summer driving around the country, camping out of my little Honda and exploring, mostly checking out the ski areas in Utah and Colorado, resorts like Sundance, Park City, Alta, Snowmass, Highlands, Steamboat—well, you get the picture.

In a way, I think I was looking for a place to settle down, for I knew I wasn't going back to school. I purposely stayed away from the ritzier places like Aspen and Vail, for I knew I couldn't afford to live there, unless I slept in my car.

After all that, I landed in Telluride that fall, even though it was quickly getting a reputation as a playground for the rich, just like Vail and Aspen. But I loved it there, and I'm sure it was because it reminded me of home, as it was a lot like Silverton. But that wasn't the only reason—I loved the diversity of slopes there—all the way from the intermediate mogul-strewn Misty Maiden to the black-diamond Plunge, which dropped you straight into town in the most direct and knee-buckling way imaginable.

Telluride has what skiers call steep and deep—steep runs and deep powder. Much of it is close to 12,000 feet in altitude, a real game changer for people from the flatlands. I've seen many a skier suffering from altitude sickness, and I guess I felt a little bit elite being able to not only survive, but to thrive there.

I was soon working a job as a lift attendant, happy as a clam, skiing every spare minute I could—the stereotypical life of the ski bum.

I'd been there a couple of years when a job as a cat operator opened up, and I jumped on it. Instead of standing all day in one spot dealing with skiers, I'd be on my own in perfect solitude, crawling in a snowcat all over the mountain, grooming the slopes after everyone else had gone home.

I didn't care for the idea of working through most of the night, but I did like the idea of being on my own with nobody looking over my shoulder. I could cruise around in my own little bubble listening to music.

As I learned the ropes, I got to where I really enjoyed the job, and I developed a camaraderie with my fellow cat operators, even though we typically didn't see each other much, each having our own section of the mountain to groom. The ski area offered two shifts—3 p.m. to midnight, and midnight to 9 a.m.—and I always chose the late-night shift because it let me see the sunrise. Sunsets could be nice, but there's nothing like a sunrise over the San Juan Mountains. Plus I liked going home when the skiers were arriving for the day.

After a number of years at this, I'd worked my way up to being the head groomer, which wasn't really all that hard to do, given there was a pretty good turnover. Most of the guys found they didn't really like working at night and didn't come back after their first season. One of our best groomers was a woman named Molly who stuck around for several seasons, saying she was there because it was a good way to get away from her husband, which we thought was just a joke until she finally divorced him and headed for greener pastures.

I'd been a groomer for maybe five years or so when my boss called me into his office and showed me a picture of a fancy new cat, asking me how I would like to drive one like it. I shrugged my shoulders, not realizing it was a big deal, as I thought it was just a new snowcat he was buying for the fleet, though it did have an odd spool-like thing on its top. By then, Telluride was well on its way to worldwide recognition for its steep and deep and had plenty of cash.

My boss, who I'll call Ron, told me, "This is a winch cat, Johnny, a PistenBully, and we're going to buy one. It costs almost a quarter-million dollars, and it'll make grooming slopes like the Plunge a lot safer. I want you to operate the thing, since you have a lot of experience. It has a 350 horsepower engine. You can play all night on this beautiful machine."

I laughed at the thought of playing while grooming steep slopes as they required a lot of concentration, though I had to admit I had the best job on the mountain. It was very satisfying to look at one of my runs when the sun came up and see the beautiful carpet of corduroy I'd created during the night.

"How does the darn thing work?" I asked. "It must be pretty special to be worth that much."

(I'll add that these machines now go for almost a half-million dollars, and the ski area now has 20 winch cats.)

"See that spool thing? That's called a turret winch. It houses several thousand feet of braided steel cable, and a steel boom plays the cable out away from the cabin. It was originally designed to pull ocean liners into docks, and they use them in logging, too. You hook the cable to an anchor, and it holds the cat back at a constant pressure so it doesn't slide when you're going down the slope. Then when you turn around, the winch pulls you back up to your anchor. The cable's very dangerous, so you don't want anyone around."

I was now impressed, and when the cat finally arrived, I spent some time training on it, then went to work. It was way different driving the darn thing down the mountain from the previous cat I'd used, where you just kind of slid down to the bottom, hoping to keep things in a state of controlled chaos. The winch cat made things much easier and safer. Now, when I basically stood on the dash while going down a steep slope into the black void of darkness, I no longer wondered if I was going to crash and burn and wake up dead.

It took me awhile to get used to the control panel, which was like something from a sci-fi movie, a bunch of smaller buttons anchored around one big red one, which was the light for the winch brake. It had a radio like the other cats, though we pretty much only radioed other drivers when we needed help or wanted to meet up for a coffee on our break, assuming there was anyone nearby.

The one thing that really bothered me at first was that once you got to the bottom of the slope and turned around, you'd have to apply pressure to pull you back up, and the cable would whip around for a minute and violently jump out of the snow, which was very dangerous.

It could be deadly if a skier or hiker come in contact with the cable, and I'd heard a few stories about people being cut in half, though the stories had come from logging camps. The cable is difficult to see, even during daylight, and is virtually invisible at night. You for sure didn't want anyone around when using these things. The cat had a flashing strobe light on it, but I didn't figure that would mean much to someone hiking up the slope to bag a run after the lifts closed, which snowboarders in particular were prone to do.

OK, the ski area knew these things were dangerous, and while installing concrete anchors at the tops of the steep slopes they'd be used on, they also installed danger signs. They also began an information campaign to inform people about these things with warnings to stay away from them. They put warnings everywhere and even contacted the local paper to run an article about it.

By then, a lot of ski areas were using winch cats, yet the general public didn't seem to have any idea they existed. That worried me, for it was getting to be a popular thing to hike on the slopes after hours, even though it was illegal. At full tension, the cable had around 10,000 pounds of pull, and any kind of contact with that kind of high tension would ensure something got destroyed. I'd heard of a few times at other areas where a deer had accidentally run into one and been killed, and it wasn't pretty.

I was kind of regretting saying I'd operate the darn thing. I have to admit to being one of those who don't care for change, which is partly why I was a cat operator to begin with. I liked the constancy of doing the same thing, no surprises. It didn't pay all that well, but I loved the lifestyle, and for me it was simple and rewarding in ways that money can't buy. I loved the solitude and the beauty of the outdoors, and like I said earlier, the sunrise over the big peaks. There was nothing like it.

I also liked the idea that I was doing something constructive, even if it was as simple as making someone's day enjoyable. I took a lot of pride in grooming the slopes, knowing that skiers would be less likely to get injured by hitting some unseen trap of hard ice.

So, I became Telluride's first winch cat operator, and as the ski area grew, there were soon a number of us. We did slopes like the Plunge, Bushwacker, and the incredibly steep runs like Silvercloud and Majestic in Revelation Bowl. Over the years, I was privileged to see thousands of stunning sunrises, as well as lots of deer, fox, coyote, lynx, elk, and even bears. I soon acquired an instinct and finesse for operating this powerful piece of equipment.

One night, I saw something that few have ever seen, and I will say it was the first time I questioned what I was doing and wondered if I might not want to quit.

I've had lots of scary events while grooming, from avalanches to blizzards to whiteouts where I was basically blinded while grooming near hundred-foot cliffs, to the time I was on Bushwacker when my winch cable picked up a giant chunk of ice that caved in my windshield, nearly killing me. But what I saw one late December night was the most terrifying thing I've ever encountered, whether on the mountain or off.

After dark, you can see maybe a hundred feet out the cat's window if it's a clear night, as that's about how far the headlights reach. If it's snowing, you're lucky sometimes to even see 10 feet ahead of you. You just have to trust your knowledge of the slope, and sometimes, you can't even trust that, you just have to stop and wait for it to clear off.

When it's like that, it feels like you're in a cocoon—it's just you, the plow, and the rumble of the diesel engine. You can get into a Zen-like state if you let yourself, but you really need to be aware in case something goes wrong.

The night of my strange event, the visibility was good, good enough that I knew I was seeing something different, not just a shadow or something from my imagination. Believe me, your imagination can run wild with you out there in the dark, and it makes you glad you're up in that warm cab with a good solid door, as you sure as heck couldn't outrun anything if you needed to. And I know this wasn't my imagination, because I wasn't the only one who saw it.

So, one night, I was cruising along, once again on Bushwacker, when I got a call on the radio from a fellow groomer I'll call Jim. I know he wouldn't want me to identify him, as he's still working there.

Jim sounded concerned. "Johnny, where are you?"

I replied, "I'm almost to the bottom of Bushwacker. What's up?"

"Something's headed your way."

Now this was odd. Why did he say something was headed my way instead of saying what it was? Why did he sound so uncertain?

"What is it?" I asked.

"Something you're going to want to avoid."

I knew then that he didn't want to say anything on the radio where others could be listening. That seemed strange to me, even a little ominous.

"OK," was all I could muster, kind of irritated that he wouldn't be more specific. "When's it going to get here?"

"Soon. Heads up, John," he replied. Now it seemed even more ominous.

"Roger," was all I could say.

It was a clear night with no moonlight, and I soon reached the bottom of the run, the winch cable becoming taut as I turned around, ready to go back up the mountain. I paused the machine for a moment, studying the slope above me, or what I could make of it, that is. I recall seeing blazing white stars through the limbs of the aspens and thinking it was a beautiful night. What could be coming my way?

I decided about all it could be was a deer, though they should all be down in the low country this time of year, avoiding the deep snow. Maybe it was a mountain lion, though they also typically went to the lowlands, following the deer. Could it be a bear? They were supposed to be hibernating, but it would account for the tone in Jim's voice. But why not just say there was a bear coming my way?

As I sat there, paused, the drone of the diesel engine the only sound, I saw something coming across the slope above me. It was more of a shadow, and it crossed the slope and went into the trees and was soon gone. I had no idea what it was, but I decided it must be a bear, but how in heck could it move through deep snow so easily?

I reached down and turned up the heat, for I was suddenly chilled. I felt slow and listless, like I'd just woke up from a deep sleep and needed a cup of coffee. I was now feeling uncertain, like I should maybe call it a night and go home, even though I had hours of grooming left.

Finally, after just sitting in the idling cat for awhile, I radioed Jim.

"I saw it, Jimbo. What was it?"

Radio silence.

"Come in, Jim. Johnny here."

Finally, Jim replied, "Yeah."

"What was it?"

"I'll talk to you later when we get off," Jim replied, and I knew that was all I was going to get out of him.

I finally started back up the slope, the cable now taut, helping stabilize the cat and pulling it upwards, the blade pushing the deep snow. I was spooked and kept looking back and forth at the trees along the run, wondering if whatever I'd seen was in there, waiting.

"Bears don't hang around, waiting for you to come along so they can attack," I consoled myself. "It's long gone."

When I got to the part of the slope where I'd seen the thing, I slowed way down, looking for tracks. Sure enough, huge postholes crossed the deep snow, sinking down farther than I could see in the dark, and I knew whatever it had been, it was heavy. I kept going, blading the tracks away, nervous and on edge.

Well, it was a long night, and at times I found myself sweating, even after I'd turned the heater way down. Then I'd get chilled and turn it back up. I finally decided I must be catching something. Maybe I'd have to take the next day off, though I hated to. I was proud of my reliability, but if I was catching a cold or even the flu, I would need to take care of myself.

Eventually the sky to the east began to slowly light up, and I was once again in awe of the huge mountain peaks surrounding me. There was nothing like the San Juan Mountains. Created by volcanism, they were rugged and wild, avalanche prone and intimidating.

As much as I loved the sight, there had been a number of times I'd thought about quitting and heading for the lowlands, finding a job that was safer and paid better, though I didn't know what that would be. My sister lived down the valley, miles from Telluride, and had a cute cottage and nice garden and didn't spend her winters fighting deep snow. Maybe it was time to retire from grooming and find something else.

Now putting the cat away for the day, I looked for Jim, but one of the other guys said he'd gone home early. For some reason, I didn't equate his early leaving with what we'd seen, but I later figured he must've been somewhat traumatized by it.

I went on home and ate a bite, then did my usual daily stuff and went to bed, after taking my dog Heidi for a walk. She had the yard to run around in all day, but I still liked to get her out to see something different.

I didn't sleep well, restless and waking every few hours, and after I finally got up, I decided I definitely was getting sick. I decided to call in and tell my boss I wasn't coming in that night.

Just then, Jim called. His first statement when I answered the phone was that he wasn't going to work that night. He then asked me to describe what I'd seen, and when I told him it was just a big creepy shadow, he got real quiet, then said he had another call coming in and had to go.

OK, I felt the conversation was kind of odd, as he'd hung up without saying much, other than he wasn't going to work. So much for my plan of taking a sick day—there was no way I could leave my boss in that kind of a bind.

I reluctantly got ready for work and eventually headed up to the mountain. I took along a big thermos of coffee, like I always did, but this time I added a shot of rum, which I never did. I figured it would help me feel better, assuming I really was getting a cold. The truth was, I needed it to bolster my courage.

It had snowed some during the night, nothing unusual for the high mountains, and I knew me and the other guys would have to work a bit faster than usual to make up for Jim not being there. We didn't do the really steep slopes every night unless the resort was busy or we got a lot of snow, and since it was midweek, I didn't anticipate having to go up Bushwacker. I was hoping to stick to the other slopes.

Now, I probably shouldn't say where this event occurred, as it's problematic with people knowing the ski area, and I don't want to scare people off a particular run, but in order to be completely honest, it was the Plunge. Like I mentioned earlier, this is one of Telluride's steep and deep and was Jim's responsibility, but I inherited it that night.

So, there I was again, on the winch cat, but I wasn't as nervous, not being on Bushwacker like the previous night. I figured the thing Jim and I had both seen was long gone. I was on the front of the mountain, the part right above town, so even if it was still around, I couldn't picture it wanting to have much to do with civilization. Of course, Bushwacker is also above town, but I didn't think of that at the time.

The Plunge is a beautiful run at night because you're right above the city lights, which accentuates the whole vertical nature of the mountain. It's pretty impressive, but when you're going downhill, the lights can actually interfere with what you're trying to see, making it imperative to focus on the task at hand.

Well, I navigated the cat track up to the top of the Plunge, then got out and hooked the winch up to a concrete post at the top of the run. Starting down, all I could see was what my headlight beams lit up, as the velvety darkness had swallowed up the slope, the nearby gondola nothing but faint shadows on the blue-white snow.

I gradually made my way down to the bottom of the slope, the snowcat blade leveling the snow. I then started uphill again, pushing snow back up to replace what the skiers had brought down with them, the cat's rear tiller leaving a perfect corduroy strip. I was feeling better, getting into the cadence of grooming, enjoying the quiet of the night, stars hanging over me like diamonds.

Back on top again, I stopped, thinking maybe it was time for some of that rum and coffee, pouring a cup from my thermos. I leaned back, wondering what time it was, when I felt something slam into the cat. At first, I thought it was a chunk of ice, like the time I mentioned earlier when one had fallen from the winch cable and taken out my windshield, but I soon remembered I was at the top of the slope and the cable was wound up in the turret.

I unbuckled my seatbelt so I could better turn around, trying to see what was behind me, when I felt the cat lurch forward. Now, since a cat's on tracks, they don't just lurch forward like a car might if pushed hard from behind, so this was a new sensation for me. I finally deduced that the slope was slipping and I was in an avalanche, which made no sense, since there wasn't an avalanche run above, just more groomed slopes going all the way to the top of the mountain, where a restaurant stood.

But the machine was definitely moving, sliding, like in an avalanche, and I felt helpless. After a brief moment, I saw the cause—it was Jim's creature! It was pushing the cat, and how in hellsbells could it push something so heavy through the snow? It must be incredibly strong.

It now moved from behind me to the side of the cat and stepped up on the platform where I could see it clearly, though only from the feet up to its waist. It was huge! Its muscular legs were as big around as a tree, and long flowing hair encased them, all matted with chunks of ice.

The machine had now slid to the very edge of where the Plunge starts, and as it teetered above the brink, I could feel myself falling forward out of my seat. I pushed myself back until I was able to buckle my seatbelt, and just in time, as the cat now tilted forward into the darkness, feeling like it was dropping off a cliff.

I don't know how, but I managed to keep my wits about me enough to engage the winch, which slowed the cat with a lurch, sending the beast flying. It soon regained its feet, and it was then that I noted it was carrying something small and white, though I couldn't make out any details.

All I could think of was getting back up and off the steep slope, so I quickly swung the cat back around. The beast ran around to the front as if to stop me, and I knew if it could basically push the cat off the edge, it was powerful enough to break through the windshield.

It was then that I saw its face for the first time, lit up by the powerful headlights of the cat. Its eyes seemed to reflect the bright light, and its face was only partly covered in hair, its cheeks and forehead dark skin. Its head was as big as a large bull's, and it looked furious. I knew then I was probably going to meet my demise, right there on the slopes of my beloved San Juan Mountains.

Now it jumped onto the edge of the blade, balancing there, still carrying something white in its hand. I was in shock, but I managed to grab the joystick that lifted the blade just as the winch cable began tightening, which whipped up just as the creature fell off, losing its balance.

I can't describe the feeling that hit me when I realized that the reason I suddenly couldn't see was because my windshield was covered with something that looked suspiciously like blood. I realized the cable had hit the beast, and I knew it hadn't stood a chance.

And even though I knew it was fortuitous for me, as the creature apparently wanted to kill me, I still felt sick.

The cat slowly moved upward until I stopped near the concrete post, and even though I was afraid, I got out and disconnected the cable. I wanted nothing more than to get out of there, and I did, not stopping until I'd reached the run above the Plunge called See Forever.

There, I waited for the sunrise, which I knew was only an hour away. I wanted to radio someone and tell them what had happened, but I knew they would say I was crazy. Not to mention I'd spilled my rum and coffee all over myself when the cat had lurched, and I smelled like alcohol. Nobody would believe me, and I might even get fired.

Finally, as the first rays began to light up the mountainside, I gathered up the courage to get out of the snowcat and see if there was any damage, which there wasn't. I then began wiping the blood off the windshield with handfuls of snow until it was all gone. I knew I needed to go back to the Plunge and see what was there, especially before they opened the lifts and someone else came along, but it was the last thing I wanted to do.

My thermos still had plenty of rum and coffee in it, so I sat there and drank it all, trying to muster up my courage. Finally, I turned and started back to the Plunge, again hooking up the winch, then slowly starting down the steep slope.

It was now light enough to see quite a ways ahead, and I soon saw a splotch of something dark on the slope. I knew it was where the creature had encountered the cable. I steeled myself for what I would find, not sure what to do if it was indeed a body.

Had it been the legendary Bigfoot? I'd heard a few stories through the years, but I'd always laughed, saying people had overactive imaginations. Would I be the first to be able to produce a body? I had no interest in this, even if it brought fame and fortune, especially if it brought fame. I had no desire to be famous, and getting rich through killing something didn't seem very positive. I knew that if I did find a body, I would somehow hide it in the trees and be quiet about it the rest of my life.

I gritted my teeth, balancing myself against the dashboard, wondering how I'd ended up in such a predicament. I should've taken the day off, like Jim did. He was obviously smarter than I was, though I knew he'd seen the creature, which I hadn't, other than as a shadow. If I'd seen what he had, I knew I would've stayed home, like he did.

Finally at the dark spot, I could now see it was deep red. It had to be blood. The last thing I wanted to do was get out of the cab, which was dangerous with the cable under tension, so I carefully turned the cat, trying to examine it from the cab.

I was stunned when I finally came upon a mangled dead rabbit, but nothing else. Had that been what the creature was carrying? Had it been hunting when I'd come along in the winch cat, interrupting its dinner?

Seeing nothing but the rabbit, I bladed it deep in the snow where no one would come across it until spring, when the ski area would be closed. I then sighed, turned around, and crept back up the slope, where I unhooked the cable and called it a day, going on home after leaving the winch cat back at the shed.

I don't remember anything at all about the following day except feeling extremely fatigued, and I finally called in sick. Ron said that Jim was still out, and I knew he'd have to drive a cat himself that night, but hey, he was getting paid for that kind of thing, making the big bucks, right? For some reason, I didn't even care.

Actually, I think I fell into a deep depression, for nothing mattered to me for weeks afterward, and I never went back to work, using up all my sick leave. If it hadn't been for taking Heidi out every day, who knows where my mind would've ended up? When my sick leave ran out, I finally called in and quit, which made me feel like a real loser, but I knew there was no way I could ever go out on those slopes again.

Well, without a job, things began spiraling downward fairly quickly, and it wasn't long before I was living with my sister, unable to pay my rent. But getting out away from the big peaks probably saved my life, for I gradually began to get better, taking Heidi out and going fishing on the nearby river every day. I spent the summer mostly by the river with Heidi, getting on food stamps so I could at least feed myself. I know my sister was beginning to wonder if I'd ever try to get another job.

That fall, I got a call from Ron, asking if I'd consider coming back. I guess Jim had eventually talked to him, explaining what he'd seen, and Ron now understood why I'd quit. Jim had stuck it out, and I will say I have to admire him for that.

I'd been missing the big peaks, and I told Ron that, but I really didn't think I could ever groom again, unless it was during the day, and that's not when the grooming was done. But Ron had decided he had a spot for me anyway. He wanted me to come work as an equipment mechanic, to service and repair the grooming machines. He wanted to know if I had any experience in hydraulics, transmissions, or welding.

I just laughed, saying, "Ron, you know I've worked up there since I was basically a kid. Where in heck would I learn all that?"

"You'll basically work in the shop and have a regular schedule, be off the mountain before dark," he replied, ignoring me. "We'll train you under the lead mechanic and send you to the PistonBully service school. When can you start?"

I was surprised, yet it felt good to know he felt like he did, especially since I'd basically walked off the job.

"I appreciate the offer, Ron. Give me a couple of days to think about it."

I hung up and called Jim. Now remember, I hadn't talked to him since the day he called me to warn me up there on the slopes that something was coming my way. We'd talked briefly on the phone that evening, then he'd said he had another call coming in and hung up.

He didn't seem at all surprised to hear from me, and when I finally got around to asking him why Ron would offer me a job after all this time, especially doing something I wasn't even qualified to do, he replied, "Johnny, you know more than you think. There were lots of times you had to troubleshoot and repair things out there on the slope. You do well under pressure, especially when you know if you can't fix it the slope won't get groomed and you may have to wait a few hours for a ride from another cat. You'll do fine. Just take the job and get back up here. We need you. Besides, you'll double your salary. Mechanics make good money."

Well, I was even more puzzled when I hung up from talking to him. The ski area was a business. They didn't have much loyalty to anyone beyond what an employee could do for them. And it went both ways. If a groomer were to be offered a higher salary at another resort, they would probably take it. Why was Ron eager to hire me back, and why did Jim seem to be supportive of it?

After giving it some thought, I decided to take it, and I was soon working in the shop. It didn't take long to get up to speed, since most everything I did was pretty straightforward. I was happy to have the work, and it felt good to be employed again. I soon had my own place again.

But I was careful to not be out and about after dark. What I'd seen had thoroughly terrified me, and my view of the mountains had changed. They were still a place of great beauty, but they no longer felt safe. When I started to miss the solitude and beauty of the mountains, I just remembered that night on the mountain.

Anyway, I seldom saw Jim, but one day he came into the shop for something or other, and we finally got to talking about that night up on the slopes. When I described what had happened, he just nodded his head, then said, "You know why Ron offered you this job, don't you?"

When I said I didn't, he replied, "It's because he saw it too. He thought he was going nuts until he asked me one day if I'd ever seen anything strange up here. When I told him we'd both seen it, he seemed really relieved. I think he wants us both around to verify he's not going insane."

"How would that work?" I asked. "He's never even asked me about it."

"He heard us talking on the radio the night I told you something was coming your way. He knows. I think it gives him some comfort to have us both here, like he's not the only one. And he understands why you walked off and felt bad about it."

I was doubtful, thinking it was an odd reason for hiring someone back, but if it gave me job security, so be it. I wouldn't argue with what had become a good paycheck.

So, Rusty, I'm now about to retire, and I always swore that before I did, I would go talk to Ron, but he's gone now. He left one morning after finishing grooming the slopes, just up and left. I'll never get a chance to ask him about things, but I guess I really don't need to. It is what it is.

When I retire, I'm moving down the valley. It's cheaper, and I want to reclaim my love of the outdoors, which is hard to do when you're always looking over your shoulder. I can do that if I get away from the big peaks, where I know the creature hides out.

Is the creature still out there? Who knows? But if it is, I hope it stays away from the winch-cat cables.

The San Juan Mountains cover a huge area, and there's room for everyone, but if this thing is what they call a Bigfoot, it should stay as hidden as possible, for its own safety, as well as the peace of mind of us humans.

2
KINTLA LAKE

I met Rose at a chili dinner fundraiser sponsored by our local search and rescue group in our town park. My wife, Sarah, was with me, and when Rose asked if she could join us at our picnic table, we of course said yes. As a ranger from Glacier National Park, Rose was there to give a talk on swift-water rescue.

We got to visiting, and she eventually told us this story, which I found very interesting, though chilling. If you like stories about Glacier, you'll enjoy my book "Glacier Bigfoot Campfire Stories." This story would fit right in, except I heard it after the book was finished. In any case, mind your P's and Q's if you ever decide to visit Kintla Lake in Glacier National Park.
—Rusty

Rusty and Sarah, I think I may have set a record for the longest time quietly floating on a log in Kintla Lake, which is ironic, as I was fleeing from something very strange.

Kintla Lake, if you've never been there, is one of Glacier National Park's hidden treasures. It's on the west side of the park and takes some effort to get to, which means the casual tourist types aren't usually found there, and unlike some of the other lakes in the park, motorized boats of any kind aren't allowed.

This makes it a quiet paradise, at least until you realize you're not the only one attracted to it. And by that, I don't mean other humans and such, but something that I didn't even know existed until one fateful day in late August, when my world was changed forever. I've also since found out that several people have gone missing there, simply disappearing with no trace.

I'm originally from Minnesota, Land of Lakes, so it makes sense that I would grow up loving the water. My parents took me and my sister canoeing pretty much as soon as we could walk, and we both became avid swimmers and canoers.

My sister actually won some state records for swimming in college, but even though I was a good swimmer, I wasn't competitive. I might add that being a good swimmer saved my life, though not in the way one would typically imagine.

I never finished college, mostly because I couldn't sit still long enough, and I was lucky to make it through high school. My friends all said I was hyperactive, but the truth was I could sit still for hours when in a canoe. It seemed like I simply couldn't calm my mind and concentrate on anything unless I was out in the natural world, and then I became like a monk and could meditate with the best of them.

So, what do you do with someone who can't bear to be indoors sitting still? I mean, I've been like this since I was a little kid. Well, my mom in her infinite wisdom—and it may sound like I'm kidding, but I'm not—decided I needed some kind of activity that would keep me busy, and since I liked to swim, she thought that maybe I should become a swimming instructor.

The main problem with this idea was that there was no pool in our little town. There were no kids' swimming programs or anything like that, so where and who would I instruct? It's kind of funny in retrospect, but finally, in lieu of teaching swimming, my mom decided I should teach people to dive. There was even less of a demand for this than for swimming, but there actually was a small dive school in town, so she talked me into enrolling when I was in high school.

My dad thought it was funny, though he agreed it would be something that would suit me, since I would be kind of like a fish, moving all the time. They forgot there were no diving jobs in our area, but that didn't matter, I soon learned to love diving and was happy.

What does all this have to do with Kintla Lake in Glacier National Park? Well, there's a progression that led me there, as you'll see. First, after burning out in college, I moved to Hawaii, where I got certified as a dive instructor in a place where there actually is a demand for such.

My parents loved that I lived there, as they could visit, but what they didn't know was that I was getting certified to do rescue work, which can be dangerous.

I finally got a job as a diving instructor with a dive shop, and I eventually volunteered with a search and rescue team based on the North Shore and even did some rescues that involved the Coast Guard. I was learning a lot, but I also had fun, spending my free time exploring with friends and looking for underwater wrecks. We actually found a Japanese plane that had been shot down near Pearl Harbor.

I loved Hawaii, but I was getting tired of being broke, as the job paid very little, relying mostly on tips. So, when I saw an opening for a ranger with water-rescue experience for the Park Service, I applied. I was ready for something new, especially the part with a regular salary.

It had been a long path, but I was soon in Glacier National Park, the land of deep glacial lakes and fast water, working as a ranger. I'm sure my mom had no idea that her early recognition of a profession suitable for my restlessness would end up taking me to a national park, and she was very happy for me, as was my dad.

Once I arrived in Montana, my first assignment was to get trained in swiftwater rescue techniques. I quickly became adept at this, as I'd developed an innate understanding of how water works and had no fear. I'd had plenty of emergency training while in Hawaii, and I quickly learned that water is the number one cause of fatalities in Glacier National Park, especially after my first "rescue" was actually the body recovery of a young guy who'd fallen into the cold icy waters in one of the park's many rivers.

But I wasn't prepared for the existence of a number of dive clubs right there in Montana. Dive in Montana? Where would you dive? Well, I was told that there were lots of places, but that Glacier was one of the most popular with its clear unpolluted lakes with some of the best underwater visibility in the West.

Even though I was a bit cocky and thought I knew a lot, I soon found that high-altitude diving was different from ocean diving and I had a lot to learn. For example, one of the more popular dive spots in Glacier is Lake McDonald, with an altitude of 3,153 feet. At altitudes like this, the pressure change is more intense, particularly during the first 30 feet of the dive, as dive gear is calibrated for sea level. And the water is so cold that one needs a drysuit.

I was soon involved with the local dive club, and among the areas where you can dive in Lake McDonald, Apgar Village became one of my favorites. It's easy to access and is home to the Pitchfork Forest, which is an underwater "forest" of rakes, hoes, shovels, axes, and, of course, pitchforks.

The forest has an interesting history. In the early days of the park, before people became more ecologically aware, taking out the trash at the end of the tourist season in the late fall meant dragging the trash out onto the ice, where it would sink when the ice melted in the spring, carrying it all out of sight. When people began diving there, they stuck all the sunken tools upright into the mud on the bottom of the lake, creating the forest. It's kind of funny how divers get into exploring this old trash and have even given it a name. I was also told that some of the tools came from when they were building the Going to the Sun Road.

OK, so one day, while I was hanging out with some of my friends from the dive club, someone mentioned how another friend had gone diving up at Kintla Lake and really enjoyed it. It was so quiet they hadn't even used diver-down flags, as the lake didn't allow motorized boats.

What's a diver-down flag? Well, when you dive at a place where there might be motorized boats, you're required to put a diver-down flag in the water. This is a rectangular red flag with a white diagonal stripe that indicates the presence of a submerged diver. It's meant to keep boats away from your dive spot as a safety measure.

Several of us talked about going up to Kintla when we had some time off. The dirt road getting there was long, windy, and rough, so we wanted to maximize our time by taking several days. We could stay at the small campground there.

In the meantime, I'd joined the local sheriff's rescue dive team as a volunteer. The sheriff's dive team was often called on to help in Glacier rescues, and I knew I could serve as a liaison between both entities. It would also give me more experience while helping with county rescues, most of which were in Flathead Lake or the Flathead River.

Oddly enough, it was at a county SAR (search and rescue) meeting that I first heard about the strangeness at Kintla Lake. I'm not sure what to call it, but I guess the word strangeness works, as it was definitely odd.

Now, as you might guess, the people who volunteer for SAR are typically a pragmatic and logical bunch, competent in the outdoors and not given to rumors and such. So when I heard about this strangeness, I gave it more credence than I might have had it come from a different source. And given how few people actually went to Kintla, it seemed unlikely to be the center of some weird rumor, unlike a place like Lake McDonald, where lots of people supposedly think they've spotted things like a lake monster like Nessie.

Keep in mind that Kintla Lake has the most remote frontcountry campground in Glacier National Park, approximately 40 rough miles from the West Entrance and near the Canadian border. The campground is for tent campers only, and its 13 sites are rarely filled, giving a sense of solitude. The lake itself is the fourth largest lake in the park at over eight miles long and is surrounded by towering mountains.

Like I mentioned earlier, it's a canoe and kayaker's paradise. Most tourists in Glacier don't even know it exists.

Well, the sheriff's SAR group knew all about Kintla, and one particular evening, after the weekly meeting had ended, a few of the group stuck around, talking about a rescue they'd been on a few days before. I couldn't help but listen in as a fellow named Joe was talking. I knew he'd been on the team a long time.

He said, "Look, I've been to Kintla lots of times, and this was different. I've never seen anything like it. After the rescue, the campground literally emptied out. The only one left was Dave, and he said he was thinking about leaving, too."

"Dave said that?" A member named Sam asked. "If he was ready to leave, it wasn't a rumor. He's been there over 20 years. He knows Kintla like nobody on the planet. He's seen it all—rogue grizzlies, summer blizzards, drunk campers, you name it."

I wasn't sure who Dave was, but I suspected he was the fellow who manned the ranger station at the lake. He'd been there forever and was highly regarded. I continued listening, wanting to learn more, especially since my diver friends and I were planning our Kintla trip.

"Did anyone ever find the guy's pack?" Someone asked.

Joe replied, "Jeff and I hiked up the lake a ways looking for it. We found the guy's compass and maps and his tent in the middle of the trail. The tent was shredded, but no pack."

Sam asked, "Do you think he actually was attacked?"

Joe said, "He had the wounds to prove it. We were ready to airlift him out by chopper, but he didn't want us to because of the cost."

"How's he doing now?" Asked another member.

Joe replied, "I think he's still in the hospital. He'll have a few scars, but his main problem is going to be mental, if you know what I mean."

"And he said it wasn't a bear?" Asked Sam.

"He was adamant it wasn't."

"What the heck else could it be? A mountain lion?"

"Who knows? But it wasn't his imagination."

I was puzzled. That particular rescue had been one of the topics of that night's meeting, as such meetings always did a recap of the previous week's activities, but no one had mentioned anything strange until now, though I had noticed a few sidelong looks during the discussion. I wanted to ask a few questions, but the guys were now leaving. I did manage to catch Joe.

"You think it's safe to go diving in Kintla this coming weekend?" I asked. I could tell from his reply that he wasn't a diver.

"Diving? Not much diving in there that I know of," he replied. "It's too darn cold."

"We wear drysuits," I said. "But I'm thinking more about what you guys were just mentioning. I mean, I overheard you talking just now, and I'm curious if you think there's something we should be aware of before camping up there."

Joe paused for a few moments, then said, "Rosie, I know you're fairly new to this area, and I respect your abilities, but you couldn't pay me enough to go camping at Kintla right now. I grew up here in Kalispell, and I've hiked a lot of Glacier's backcountry, and I truly believe there's something out there that wasn't there a few years ago. I can't tell you what it is, but a number of us have felt its presence. I personally think it came in from Canada."

I frowned, then asked, "What is it?"

Joe shook his head. "I just told you I don't know what it is."

I wasn't going to give up. "What do you *think* it is?"

"If I told you and word got out, it would ruin my reputation. I'm not going to say what I think it might be, but let's just say it's not human and it's not a regular-type mammal. Just do me a favor and don't go up to Kintla—or if you decide to ignore my advice and go anyway, let me first put you in touch with that poor guy in the hospital."

"Was he seriously injured?"

"He had some good cuts on his legs that I'm sure needed a lot of stitches, but his main injury seemed to be mental. He was hysterical when we got to him. Ranger Dave heard him screaming and radioed out, then went and found him. The guy actually tried to strangle

Dave, thinking he was whatever had been after him. If some other campers hadn't come along, he might've succeeded. They all had the guy pinned to the ground when we got there. Just do me a favor and go to Bowman instead. It's just as pretty and easier to access."

I thanked him, and we all left. As I drove back home to West Glacier, I felt a strange sense of puzzlement combined with a fear I'd never felt before. Growing up in Minnesota, I'd spent lots of time out in the deep woods totally alone, usually in a canoe. I'd never felt fearful, and we have bears and gray wolves up there, lots of both. I'd had wolves serenade my remote campsites more than once.

And I will say we'd heard stories of Bigfoot—could that be what Joe was talking about? It seemed ludicrous. I knew Bigfoot was just folklore, something people talked about late at night to scare themselves, but something strange did seem to be going on.

The next day at lunch, I mentioned what I'd heard to a fellow Glacier employee, also a diver planning on going to Kintla with us. Her name was Tracy, and she was an interpretive ranger, one who deals with educating the public about the park. She laughed, saying she'd heard tales of Bigfoot in the park before, but never anything definitive. Like me, she wasn't a believer, and she'd worked in Glacier for over a decade. I figured if anyone would know, it would be her.

So, we went ahead with our planning, and Friday evening, off we went on the long dusty drive to Kintla Lake. There were six of us in two vehicles. We'd camp through the weekend, returning home late Sunday evening, which would give us two days of diving. Needless to say, none of us had ever dived there.

It was a long drive, and when we got there, it had started raining. What the heck? The weather report had called for a sunny weekend, but I've since learned that the weather in the high Rockies of Glacier can be anything it wants to be with no notice. We quickly pitched our tents and crawled inside as a deep fog came in off the lake, leaving everything damp and wet. I managed to boil water for tea on my little campstove and ate some cold pizza I'd brought.

I'd noticed that the ranger station was locked up, and with the bars over its windows, it looked inhospitable. Tracy told us that Dave had put the bars up after a grizzly had broken in one winter, trashing everything. We had no idea where Dave had gone, but we figured he'd probably gone out to resupply.

I hadn't noticed anyone else in the campground, and it all seemed lonely and forlorn. It was the end of August, and we knew winter came early to the north country, but we really didn't expect it so soon, though I noticed the grasses had all turned yellow. It all felt really wild, and I actually even toyed with the idea of talking everyone into going home.

Well, everybody else seemed to be having a good time, hanging around in their tents playing cards or whatnot, so eventually I went to bed, not wanting my depressing mood to put a damper on their fun.

At first, I couldn't get warm, the damp air seeming to seep into my down bag, but I eventually fell asleep. I don't know what time I woke, but it felt like the deepest part of the night. I lay there for awhile, not really sure where I was for awhile, then waking up and realizing I needed to pee.

Darn! This was the worst part of camping, having to get out of a warm bag and crawl out into the darkness. I waited as long as I could, feeling kind of leery about going out into the wilderness just outside my tent. But I finally had no choice, so I slipped out of my bag and quietly unzipped the tent, climbing out.

I was shocked by what I saw! The entire night sky was lit up! The fog had lifted, and what I saw was absolutely indescribable! I could see a thick blanket of silver stars against an emerald-green sky, and I knew the Northern Lights would soon begin. I'd seen them like this before in Minnesota, the lights preceded by a green sky.

I was mesmerized, wondering if the draped curtains of the Aurora would soon appear, and not wanting to go back into my tent, I leaned against a small tree, looking straight up into the equinox.

Suddenly, I heard a twig snap, and I knew I wasn't alone. By then, my eyes had become more used to the dark, and I could make out the shape of a dark form over by one of the other tents. I held my breath, wondering what it was.

Now I heard someone whisper, "Rosie, that you?"

I sighed, relieved. It was Tracy. As I answered, she made her way over to where I stood.

"I heard something odd and can't go back to sleep. Did you hear it? Maybe 10 minutes ago."

I told her I hadn't heard anything, but was now wondering if that hadn't been what had awakened me.

"What did it sound like?"

"At first I thought it was a wolf, but then it got really weird."

"Weird?"

"Yeah, it sounded like something being choked, a gurgling sound."

"Maybe a wolf drowned in the lake," I replied, puzzled.

"It was too loud to be a wolf. It sounded like it was way across the lake. A wolf's call wouldn't carry like this did."

"Wow," was all I could muster to say, now thinking of what Joe had said. "Did it scare you?"

Tracy hesitated, then said, "It made me want to get out of here. I feel like maybe we're in some kind of danger."

Just then, the Aurora began the display I'd been waiting for, huge curtains of green with edges of red and gold moving and swaying in the sky. We both stood in awe, the howling sound forgotten for the moment.

After a good 10 or 15 minutes, the fact that it was the middle of the night and also cold began to catch up to me, and I said, "Tracy, I have to go back to bed. Let's just wait and see how we feel tomorrow. If you hear anything, come and wake me, or better yet, wake everybody. Maybe it was just a loon or something."

"It wasn't a loon, Rosie."

I nodded my head as Tracy headed back to her tent, then I felt a sudden sense of panic and climbed back into my tent. I lay there for awhile, listening, and next thing I knew, it was daylight.

I crawled out of my tent to find everyone else up and making breakfast, a beautiful blue sky overhead. It looked like a perfect day for diving. Tracy looked totally relaxed, like her fears from the previous night had been her imagination. Maybe I'd dreamt it all.

As we sat at a picnic table eating pancakes, a thin older man in a ranger uniform came walking up, and I knew it was Dave. He'd just returned from town, he told us, and wanted to say hello, making his rounds, checking out the campground. He confirmed that we were the only ones there.

Pointing out what appeared to be new snow on the high peaks surrounding the lake, he told us it wouldn't be long before the campground was closed, and he'd go back to Colorado where he spent the winters with his family.

As everyone else got their dive equipment ready, I fiddled with mine, tired and unenthusiastic, feeling like I wanted to go home. Dave had started pulling weeds, but seeing me sitting there, he came over and sat down across from me.

"You kids are going diving, right?" He asked. "We don't get many divers here. Off the south shore, if the light's just right, you can see a sunken boat. I know it's not real old because it has green paint on it. If you guys get out there, take a dip and tell me what it is."

I told him that seeing how the south shore was a good ways away, I doubted if we'd get out that far.

"Well," he added, "The boat's in about 30 feet of water. I saw it from a canoe once. I sure would like to know more about it. I've been here many years and never had divers come along where I could ask. Have you seen the Shovel Fork Forest over at Lake McDonald?"

"You mean the Pitchfork Forest?" I asked.

"It used to be called the Shovel Fork Forest," he replied. "Things change. But say, Tracy said you also work for the park. Did you hear anything about our latest rescue over here?"

I sighed. I was actually trying to forget about it, as I suspected it was why I had no enthusiasm for diving. I told Dave what Joe had told me.

"I'm surprised Joe would mention something like that," Dave replied, but when I told him I was a member of the county SAR team, he nodded his head.

"I've been a ranger here for 20 years, though I actually started out as a camp host," Dave said. "And last night was the first time I've ever felt uncomfortable spending the night here. I actually drove down to Polebridge and camped in my pickup. If I'd known you kids were coming in, I would've stayed. I just didn't want to be here alone. You kids be careful. You know what I'm talkin' about."

Dave was gone before I could tell him I actually *didn't* know what he was talking about. All I knew is what Joe had said about something strange going on.

I shrugged my shoulders, then went and got my dive gear ready, even though diving was the last thing I wanted to do right then. But everyone else was raring to go, so I decided to go along. It was either that or spend all day sitting at that picnic table.

We found a good place to get into the water, not far from the campground, and by then things had warmed up considerably. The water was a rich turquoise blue, and I could see how, when the sun was high, the light could filter down to where one could see the boat Dave had mentioned, it was so clear.

I knew that at over 400 feet deep, Kintla was deeper than most Montana lakes. I'd seen photos of the lake, and as one travels farther up it, the mountain slopes dive straight into the water and on down into its mysterious depths.

I'd read that the name Kintla came from the Kutenai word for "sack," and Kutenai legend said that many had drowned there. The lake was like a sack—once you got in, you couldn't get out. It actually was all beginning to creep me out, beautiful or not.

For the first time in my life, I questioned whether or not I wanted to be a diver. I just can't describe how I felt that day. It was like nothing I've felt before or since. I looked at Tracy, wondering if she felt the same way, but she was laughing and excited to get into the water.

Well, I finally made up my mind to enjoy the day, though I pretty much simply followed everyone else around. I felt very low energy and was happy when we stopped for lunch. We hadn't found much, but just cruising around the lake had been OK.

After lunch, everyone decided they wanted to go for a hike and take photos of the beautiful high peaks. I was still feeling lackluster, so I decided to stay at camp. It wasn't long before everyone was gone, leaving me sitting once again at the picnic table. Their voices faded into the distance, and I was glad for the quiet.

But it seemed that the longer I sat the more unsettled I became. I finally got up and walked to the ranger station to see if Dave was around, but it was once again closed up, his pickup gone. I wondered if he'd again driven to Polebridge. It didn't seem like him, since he now had people in the campground. He struck me as a very conscientious guy.

I looked back towards my tent, and that's when I thought I saw movement in the trees. I stood still for awhile, then realized it was a deer. It stood watching me, then eventually turned and walked slowly back into the forest.

I was beginning to wish I'd gone with the others, yet I still felt tired. Thinking that maybe a cup of hot chocolate would wake me up, I got out my little stove, setting it on the picnic table. Soon realizing my matches were damp from the fog, I walked over to Tracy's pickup, as I knew she had some in her glove box.

The truck was locked, which I found somewhat disconcerting. I guess she hadn't been thinking I might need to get inside and had locked it out of habit. I was now kicking myself for not bringing my own vehicle. I felt vulnerable without the protection, especially in bear country, and if it rained or there was lightning, a vehicle was a good place to hole up.

OK, no hot chocolate for me. I stood there for awhile, kind of out of it, then crawled into my tent and stretched out, deciding to take a little nap. I was still tired from getting up in the middle of the night, and besides, there wasn't anything else to do.

I lay there for awhile, wondering when the others would come back, and instead of going to sleep, I started feeling restless. I don't know how to describe it, except to say it felt as if I were being watched by something threatening.

I suddenly started feeling claustrophobic in the tent, like I needed to get out so I could see what was around me. I'd left my dive gear on the picnic table to dry out, so I crawled out and went and sat by it, feeling some strange sort of attachment to it, a sort of comfort. It felt kind of like a touchstone, like something familiar. I know that sounds strange, but I was now feeling really out of my element.

I began to think of the backpacker Joe had helped rescue, and how Joe had said the guy was mentally disturbed—was the power of suggestion now affecting me? I had no logical reason for feeling so uneasy.

I now wanted nothing more than to get inside a vehicle, where I'd feel safe, so I walked over to the SUV the others had come in, but it was also locked. Man, didn't everyone know that when you're out in the backcountry you need to leave your rig unlocked in case somebody needs shelter? I found it disturbing. Of course, I would've done the same, locked my vehicle when going for a hike, but not if someone was staying behind.

I went back over to the picnic table and fiddled with my dive gear some more, feeling even more restless, talking to myself. "Get it together, there's nothing here, you're perfectly safe."

Maybe I should go for a hike, I thought. Maybe I'd meet up with the others. They couldn't be all that far away. Or maybe I should just start walking on the road out, hoping I'd meet Dave.

Now I thought I saw something out of the corner of my eye, something back in the forest. It was probably just another deer, yet I felt my insides clutch. I turned to look just in time to see something dark slip behind the trees into the shade, where I couldn't make it out.

Now, I have to say that this really bothered me, as whatever it was, it seemed as if it were being intentionally elusive. I sat there for a moment, watching, thinking it might be a bear and wondering where my bear spray was, then realizing it was locked in Tracy's pickup.

OK, now I felt even more insecure. I was a sitting duck, nobody around, no bear spray, and no place to run or hide. I leaned back, trying to relax, breathing deep, wondering why I was turning into a nervous wreck. Of course there was nothing there. As hard as I looked, I saw nothing, just shadows.

I sat very still, hoping to hear the sound of a vehicle coming, again wondering where Dave had gone. I heard something and held my breath—was that a low growl coming from the trees where I thought I'd seen the shadowy figure? Oh man, what now?

I was terrified. In retrospect, my actions reflected this—they seemed so desperate and illogical that I can't even explain what was going through my brain—all I knew was I had to flee, that my life was in danger.

I guess it was the culmination of hearing Joe talk about the backpacker and of Ranger Dave saying he'd left for the night, afraid of spending it alone out there, as well as Tracy saying she'd heard something during the night. It all came together, leaving me in a state of panic. For all my nights in the deep woods of Minnesota, I'd never felt like this.

I now desperately wished I'd listened to Joe and stayed home. I quickly slipped into my drysuit and put on my diving tank and goggles, walking along the lakeshore until the water was deep enough to swim. I then stepped into the icy lake.

I couldn't help but look back, and there it was—and it was huge! It stood looking at me, and I sensed a feeling of surprise, though that was probably just me projecting how I thought it should feel. My own feelings were beyond surprise, for this thing was standing upright and holding a large branch in a menacing way.

I knew my intuitions had been right ever since I'd come to Kintla. My subconscious was trying to protect me and get me out of harm's way. I dipped my head under the water and disappeared from sight.

Later, trying to recall what I'd seen, all I could come up with was something big and dark, something beyond description, and I knew I was repressing it for self-protection. It had caused the backpacker to go nuts, and I knew I couldn't dwell on it, as I needed my wits to survive. Even later, when I saw it again, I couldn't really process what it was, and it became a maelstrom of vague impressions. Sometimes, when I'm drifting off to sleep at night, it tries to emerge from my subconscious, but I'm too afraid to let it. That's when I wake up and can't sleep.

OK, I had no idea where I was going, I just wanted to flee. I was on automatic pilot, yet I knew I needed to get out into deep water where this thing couldn't follow me. I knew I didn't have a lot of air in my tank, and I realized I would eventually have to swim to shore and somehow make my way back to camp—or better yet, find my friends.

I swam a long ways underwater until I figured I was reaching the middle of the lake, and for the first time in my life, I was terrified to think of how deep the water below me was. I knew I had a limited amount of air in my tank, and I couldn't just come out of the lake anywhere. I had to be very careful to not meet up with this creature.

I surfaced, and looking around me, realized I was now far from the campground and coming close to the south shore of the lake, not even close to the middle. My wrist dive-computer had a GPS, but I'd left it back in my tent.

I knew that the north shore was where the trail went, eventually coming to a backcountry campground and then following Kintla Creek to Upper Kintla Lake and on over Boulder Pass. I needed to be on the north shore, not the south side, which was exactly as the Kutenai legend described it, like a sack—once you got in, you couldn't get out. Thick forest came right to the edge of the lake with no visible beaches anywhere. I would have to swim all the way across the lake to the north shore if I wanted to find a place to get out without having to bushwhack through thick forest and underbrush.

I dipped back underwater, not wanting to be seen, still feeling a sense of doom, though the panic had subsided some. It wasn't long until I came to what seemed to be an underwater forest of dead trees, all standing upright, though their branches were bare and their trunks were a ghostly white. A school of kokanee salmon wove in and out of the branches, and nearby was a deep underwater ravine.

I'd been to a similar sight in Lake McDonald where Sprague Creek enters the lake, the remnant of a forest that's still rooted, but now underwater. One ranger told me it was evidence of a past time when the lakes were much lower, and as the water had risen, it had drowned the forest, leaving it still rooted. I soon realized that I must be in shallower waters to see such a forest. I had to be reaching the shore.

Now, like I mentioned before, most lakes in Montana are cold, and in Flathead Lake, which is near Glacier, the water temperature is 45 degrees by the time you go 100 feet down. In Glacier, they're even colder, which makes sense, since most of them originate in glaciers.

Cold water poses problems for most diving gear, as your oxygen regulator can freeze up, as well as go into free-flow and not shut off, and the tiniest hole in a drysuit can make diving uncomfortable. In really cold water, divers will fill their suits with argon gas, which is a heavy, inert gas that helps insulate your body. In those conditions, most divers won't go deeper than 50 or 60 feet, and a long dive lasts only 30 minutes.

Well, I figured at this point I'd been in the lake almost an hour, and I could feel the cold beginning to seep in through my drysuit. I needed to get out and warm up, yet here I was on the south shore, no place to get out of the water without crawling through tangled tree limbs and branches and understory. And there was no trail to get back to the campground. I desperately needed to get back to the north side of the lake. How had I become so totally disoriented, given all my diving experience?

I was getting fatigued. I wasn't even sure I could swim across, yet alone negotiate the hike back. I was going to have to come out somewhere on the south shore, rest, then try to swim back.

Oddly enough, through all this, the thought that I should find Dave's underwater boat wreck for him and identify it came to mind as something I needed to do. Of course, I wasn't thinking straight and was becoming chilled, the first sign of hypothermia.

Instead of getting out of the lake, I now slowly paddled along the shore, looking for the boat. He'd said it was in about 30 feet of water, and I realized the water was getting too shallow as I was nearing the shore, so I turned and began slowly swimming back out into the lake.

It was then that I saw it—not the boat, but the black creature! It was standing along the shoreline exactly where I'd been planning on landing. It had somehow been watching me as I surfaced, making its way around the lake, trying to follow me.

And now, as I watched, it did the unthinkable—it jumped into the water and began swimming out towards me. I could see even from a distance that it had powerful arms and would soon reach me. I remember thinking it looked like a black shark, swimming up down, up down with its big strokes, and it had come quite a ways out when I finally came to my senses.

I dove down out of sight. It couldn't catch me if it couldn't see me, right? I went down to about 30 feet, then realized there was something nearby, something that was closing in on me down under the water. Having been mostly an ocean diver for a number of years, my first thought was that it was a school of fish, but as it came closer, I realized with a sinking feeling that it was the creature.

It was swimming underwater! My instinct said to go up, up, up, where I wouldn't be dependent on my equipment if something were to happen, and I quickly started for the surface, but I was tired and not moving as quickly as I normally would. Before I knew it, the creature was near me, flailing its arms at me, trying to hit me, both of us still underwater.

As I ducked, its huge hand caught my oxygen regulator and knocked it out of my mouth. To my horror, the regulator started to free-flow, whipping across my body to my left, where it was hard to see it.

Now I was just a couple of feet from the creature, facing it, and I had no oxygen, no way to breathe. Reaching for my regulator and knowing I now only had a few seconds to keep the situation from becoming deadly, I shot upwards, holding my breath until I could get the regulator back in my mouth.

Soon back at the surface, I was happy I hadn't been at a greater depth, where I would've had a serious chance of decompression sickness or possibly even a lung-over-expansion injury from surfacing too quickly. But I now had a bigger problem—the creature had also surfaced nearby, water dripping from the course hair hanging off it in long clumps.

Like I said earlier, I still can't remember what it actually looked like in detail, but I'll never forget the look in its eyes—it was less than twenty feet away, and I could clearly see its huge black pupils. It studied me for a moment, and I got the feeling it was puzzled by the sight of my dive mask and equipment, almost as if it was unsure of what I was.

I took the brief reprieve as a chance to again dive, but this time I went deeper, for I could now see the outline of something below me. It was the boat Dave had mentioned! It was on its side, and I quickly slipped under the hull, hidden.

I waited, certain the creature knew where I was, waiting for me to come out. How long could it stay underwater? Surely it needed to go up for air once in awhile. I worried that the carbon dioxide bubbles from my regulator would give me away.

I was as still as could be, but I knew I had to surface before long, as I was running out of air. Since we'd been doing fairly shallow recreational diving, I didn't have a backup tank, which I would always have when ocean diving. I needed to surface, but I knew that panicking would just make me use more air, so I tried to make my breathing slow and measured. Finally, when I could wait no longer, I began slowly surfacing.

There was no sign of the creature, and I suspected it had come up and then gone back underwater, looking for me. All I could do was start swimming for the shore as fast as possible. I quickly slipped my empty tank off and let it sink, knowing a good chunk of change was going with it, for tanks aren't cheap. I then set out for the shore, which seemed miles away.

I'd gone only a short distance when I came upon a large floating log from one of the many larch trees lining the shore. Could I climb onto it without rolling? I badly needed to rest. It was tricky, but I managed, climbing up onto it.

I stretched out and began slowly paddling along, now trying to head for the north shore, all the time looking over my shoulder for the creature. I stayed as low on the log as possible, head down, and I'll always associate the smell of wet wood with that day on Kintla Lake. I've actually developed a distaste for the smell of any kind of dampness.

I could soon see I was no match for the current, which was now taking me back to the south shore, and I started to panic, thinking I should get back into the water and swim. I knew the creature was still looking for me.

It then occurred to me that Kintla Creek, which flowed into the upper part of the lake, exited by the campground, eventually meeting up with the Flathead River miles below. There had to be a current going through the lake in that direction. Could I find it? Was it too far underwater to make any difference?

As I slowly floated along on the log, I began studying the water, and I soon found what looked to be a place farther out in the lake where leaves and smaller logs were floating more westerly. It had to be the current of the underwater stream, if only I could work my way out there.

Even though I was exhausted, I managed to push the log out farther, and sure enough, there was a current going towards the lake's outlet, which was where the campground and ranger station sat. Relieved, I was soon floating along in that direction, still wondering where the creature was. I knew I would be easy prey on the log.

I have no idea how long I floated along on that log, but it was now getting dark, the sunset lighting up the slopes of the distant mountains at the head of the lake. It was so dark that I didn't even realize when I came to the shore, thinking it was just a place where the shadows deepened, but when the log caught in some rocks, I knew I'd passed from the lake into Kintla Creek, and I crawled off the log, knowing I was near the Ranger Station.

I had no idea where the creature was, but I knew that the log had been a godsend, hiding me from below and giving me an easy way of transport, though slow.

As I stumbled along the trail to the campground, the forest shadows seemed to be hiding something mysterious and threatening, something looking for me, but I knew I was now safe.

Everyone waited at the campground, including Dave, who was about to radio out for search and rescue. I hadn't realized it, but I'd been floating along on that log for hours, and everyone had been back at camp for some time.

Tracy took down my tent and loaded my gear for me, as I was too exhausted, while Dave and the others asked me about what had happened. I didn't feel much like talking, so I just told them I'd gotten lost. That seemed to satisfy everyone, and we were soon on the road back home.

It was a quiet trip back to West Glacier until Tracy asked where my tank was, and I then decided to tell her what had actually happened. She was quiet, and I knew she was thinking about the sound that had awakened her in the night. She dropped me off at my house, helping me drag my stuff inside, and I fell into bed, where I slept a restless sleep, dreaming about strange eyes that cut through my very being.

I've since quit diving, though I still assist with swiftwater rescues. I've thought about leaving Glacier many times, but I figure as long as I don't go into the backcountry alone, I'll be OK. It's a beautiful place, and when I think of leaving, I think of how many people I've helped rescue and how that's a good thing. My job keeps me busy, preventing me from thinking too much about what I saw out at Kintla Lake.

I found out that Dave retired at the end of the season after my incident. I never got the chance to talk to him about it, but somehow, I don't think it's necessary, for I know he was well aware of what was going on—just like me and Joe and that backpacker and the others who have disappeared there.

Sometimes, when I'm out on the shore of places like Lake McDonald, I wonder how much I really don't know about the park and what's gone on in places like Kintla, though I realize I'm probably better off not knowing.

I keep watching for an opening so I can transfer to a different park, maybe someplace like Arches or Death Valley, where there's no deep water or forests for strange creatures to hide in, though I know I would miss the water. But sometimes you just have to adapt.

3

THE BURNING MOUNTAIN

This story came from a woman called Georgie who'd arranged a group fishing lesson on the Colorado River for herself and a few friends. I don't fish the Colorado very often, as it usually requires a drift boat and a very different kind of technique from the streams I prefer, but this was a one-time thing she'd put together. I guess she was kind of like a Hobbit in that she made this fishing lesson a present for everyone else on her birthday.

It actually ended up being a lot of fun, as we fished from a fairly large beach and the water was low enough that we could wade out a ways. But Georgie didn't want to wade since she couldn't swim, so I pretty much stayed on the shore with her, showing her how to fly fish.

Interestingly enough, we were fishing below the Burning Mountain of this story, and when I asked her about the burn scars I could see high on the mountainside, she told me the following. —Rusty

Rusty, I once lived here in Western Colorado, but I've since moved to the prairie. I love the mountains, but I no longer want to live here—I'm just back visiting for awhile. I had a rental here in the little town of New Castle, though most people have probably never heard of it, as it has only about 1,000 people, with nothing much to distinguish it from any other little town—well, maybe there *is* something, but I'm getting ahead of myself.

New Castle was once a coal-mining town, but the mines have been closed for many years. They closed after a couple of really bad explosions where almost 100 miners were killed. The town itself almost died off after the mines closed, but it eventually became a bedroom community for a town I'm sure you *have* heard of—Aspen. So now most everyone commutes up-valley to work for tourists and the rich.

I'm lucky, as I'm a retired teacher and the only one I have to take care of is myself—well, and my three dogs, who are getting old like me—Sammy, Shoots, and Tigger. Tigger got his name from having odd stripes around his face like a cat. Sammy and Tigger are part corgi and Shoots is a dachshund. You may think Shoots is an odd name, but it fits him, as every time you turn around he's doing something that makes you say, "Shoots!"

Even though I lived in the city limits, I was near what's called Burning Mountain. My little cottage backed to a small creek, then right across from that was the bottom of the mountain. I could see partway up its side but was too close to see the top, as it kind of towered over me. It blocked most of my view, so I got none of the wonderful sunsets most people around here can see, which sometimes really bothered me. When I'd get to feeling claustrophobic, I'd take the dogs and go for a drive.

Let me tell you a little about Burning Mountain. Everything in town is named after it—Burning Mountain this and Burning Mountain that—and it's part of what's called the Great Hogback, which stretches for at least a hundred miles across this part of Colorado, all the way from the little town of Meeker to the even smaller town of Redstone.

The Great Hogback is a huge uplift, part of which is called the Butcher Knife Ridge, just to give you an idea of what it looks like. It's basically a long narrow mountain with a serrated top. It's full of coal seams, and the few towns near it were pretty much all coal-mining towns, just like New Castle.

The Hogback is covered with juniper trees and sagebrush and lots of rocky ledges. It's a great place for wildlife, like mountain lions and marmots, and I could sit in my living room and watch redtail hawks hunting on the steep hillside. And something else I could see from my living room was a most unique feature—the place where the mountain was starting to sink from seams of coal burning inside it, which is why it's called Burning Mountain. Like its name suggests, the mountain is on fire—but deep inside.

Coal-seam fires aren't that unusual, and I've read there are thousands worldwide, some that have been burning for hundreds of years, like one in Australia. The fires can be started by lightning or wildfires or even self-combustion and generally smolder because of a lack of oxygen.

Anyway, I could see the burn scars from my living room. These are places where nothing will grow because the heat from the underlying coal-seam fire is too hot. Because the coal underneath is burning, the land has subsided a little, creating large dips in the mountainside, kind of like giant shallow sinkholes the size of a house.

The heat has turned the rocks red, and the only thing that grows is grass, and it struggles, growing in patches. A few years ago, a similar burning coal seam farther along the Hogback caught the grasses on fire, and it spread to the nearby town of Glenwood Springs, burning almost 30 houses.

No one really knows what started the fire in the seam inside the hill above my house, but it was probably one of the mining explosions. The coal here has a lot of methane associated with it, which makes it hard to mine because it's very explosive. In any case, the places where the seams beneath the surface are on fire never accumulate any snow, as it just melts off—and this accounts for, in my opinion, what I saw one cold winter day a few years ago. Let me explain.

My living room faced my back yard, and I could sit in my recliner and look out my patio door across the creek and up the side of the mountain. I liked to sit there and drink my morning coffee, as sometimes I'd see ducks or other kinds of birds come to the creek, and once in awhile, even a deer or two.

Well, it was January, the coldest month in this part of Colorado, and we'd just had a big front come through a couple of days before, which dumped a good foot of snow, and after it cleared off, it got really cold. It was one of the coldest stretches of that particular winter, getting down around minus 10 or so every night for a week or longer. I remember putting extra bird feed out, as I knew they'd need the extra calories to stay warm.

It was dawn, and I was already on my second cup of coffee, wishing the sun would hurry up and burn off the fog. I really couldn't see much, but every once in awhile the fog would drift enough that I could make out part of the mountainside. It was a desultory sight, lots of cold snow and drifting clouds. Sometimes I found the snow and fog beautiful, but that particular day it was dreary.

As I sipped my coffee, glad I was inside, the fog drifted enough that I could see one of the burn scars above me, but just for a moment. Something looked different, but it fogged back in before I could figure out why.

I kept a pair of binoculars by my chair for birdwatching, so I picked these up and waited for the fog to drift to where I could see again. After awhile, it opened up, and I focused on the scar, which was a wet dirty red from the snow melting on the red rocks. Even though it was really cold outside, the heat beneath the surface was melting the snow.

I really couldn't make out much, so I figured what I'd seen was just shadows, and I pretty much forgot about it, thinking maybe there'd been a deer or something up there, though they generally stay away from the hot areas.

Now, if you've ever been to Yellowstone, you know what a fumarole is—an opening through which hot gases emerge. Burning Mountain also has fumaroles, cracks in the surface where steam comes out when enough water trickles into the burning seam. After a good rain, you can see several fumaroles up on the mountain where the burn scars are. The steam plumes aren't all that big but are definitely visible, though they usually dissipate after a few hours.

When the fog lifted, I could see that the fumaroles up on the mountainside above me were going pretty good, and I again thought I saw something different, something dark. It looked like a dark bush by one of the fumaroles, but I knew there weren't any bushes growing there. As I watched with my binoculars, the bush moved! I thought I was seeing things!

I got up and walked to the big sliding glass door that led out to my yard and looked again, now at a little different angle. The bush was gone!

I was puzzled. Was something or someone hanging out near the warmth of the fumarole? I knew wild animals stayed away from it, so I wondered if it might be a person, maybe someone homeless, which would make sense, given how cold it was.

I checked periodically throughout the morning, but didn't see anything. After lunch, I went next door to my daughter's house, where I would babysit my five-year-old granddaughter while my daughter, Janie, who's a nurse, was at work. Her husband, Eric, was a truck driver and was often gone for a week at a time.

Sometimes my granddaughter, Chrissie, would come spend the night with me when my daughter was on the night shift and Eric was gone. They were the reason I'd moved to the little cottage after I retired, and though I often thought about moving somewhere warmer and where I could see out, I knew I would miss them too much.

Chrissie was a Sesame Street fan, and we usually had to watch an episode or two each day, and her favorite character was the Cookie Monster. She was getting to the age where kids sometimes have imaginary friends, so I wasn't a bit surprised when she informed me that the Cookie Monster had paid her a visit the previous night. She said he had come to her bedroom window in the night and watched over her as she slept.

I asked her how she knew he was there if she was asleep, and she said he'd woken her up telling her to come and open the window, but she'd gone back to sleep. After telling me this, she went back to whatever she'd been doing, coloring something or other, totally unperturbed.

I thought it was kind of cute at first, her seeing the Cookie Monster, but the more I thought about it, the more concerned I got. Had she really seen something? Had someone tried to get into her room through the window? Hearing someone talking with the window closed didn't make sense—how had she heard them?

I asked her if the Cookie Monster had been blue, but she said no, he was black. This made me even more concerned, and I gave her a talk about never opening the window or door for anyone and that she should go get her mom next time. I was very serious and hoped to make an impression on her, but she didn't seem very worried.

I told her mom about it when she got home, but for some reason, it didn't even occur to me to go outside and look for tracks in the snow under Chrissie's window. I guess I wasn't really taking it as something that had actually happened, given how kids can imagine things.

Well, that night, around 2 a.m., the dogs, who always sleep on the foot of my bed, all started growling, an odd growl that I'd never heard from any of them before. It was low, like they wanted to alert me but not let whatever they were growling at know they were there.

They're a pretty bold bunch when it comes to guarding things, but they actually seemed afraid. This was a first, as I'd once watched my dachshund, Shoots, chase a horse across a field, totally unafraid, and corgis were bred to herd cattle, which are huge compared to the little dogs.

I quietly got up and went to the living room and looked through the windows, walking all around the house, but saw nothing. Finally, ready to go back to bed, writing it off to the dogs' imaginations, I happened to look over towards my daughter's house.

There was something in her yard! It wasn't close to the house, but was instead under one of her big crabapple trees. As I watched, it sank down to the ground and rolled over onto its side, then appeared to just stay there, like it was bedded down for the night.

My daughter's house was old, just like mine, and had lots of big trees in the yard. It was a rental property with two houses, which was perfect for us. The crabapple trees were the most gorgeous things in the spring with their pinkish red blooms, and they bore lots and lots of crabapples. The birds loved them, and even the deer would come into the yard and stand on their hind legs to reach the fruit. I have some really nice pictures of a pileated woodpecker poking its beak into a crabapple and eating it.

Anyway, I went back to bed, thinking that it was a deer that had come for the crabapples and had then bedded down, a really big buck. The next morning I got up and looked out, and I could see the snow there was all packed down. What I wasn't expecting was to find the lower branches of the crabapple tree pretty much decimated.

Whatever had been there had not just stripped the branches of the crabapples, like a deer would, but had actually torn off the limbs.

Well, I can tell you, this did not make me or my daughter very happy. I called her, and we went out and looked around, and the snow was packed down under the tree like something heavy had rolled all around. I was now beginning to wonder if somehow one of the cattle from the pasture up the road hadn't escaped and got into the yard, though it didn't make sense, as it was fenced. But I knew that cattle would sometimes crawl through a wire fence if it's not barbed.

It was a bright sunny day, and other than being puzzled, I soon forgot about the torn-up tree branches and got busy doing other things. Janie had the day off, so I wasn't watching Chrissie. I did look up at the burn scars again, but saw nothing unusual, and the fumaroles had all dissipated, which was normal, as they only put out steam right after it rains or snows when water runs down into the coal seam.

That afternoon, my friend Kathy from up the street called me wanting to talk, as she often did. She was also retired and got bored, not being as good at entertaining herself as I am. During the conversation, she asked if I'd heard all the dogs barking up and down the street during the night. I told her no, but that my dogs had been upset, and something had bedded down in the yard. Kathy said that the barking had gone on for some time, and she was surprised I hadn't heard it, but I told her my house was really well insulated.

We soon got to talking about other things, and I thought no more of it. I eventually went out and cleaned up the torn branches, hauling them to the dumpster. They weren't small—some of them were three or four inches thick—and I wondered why an animal would feel it necessary to rip them off the tree. Maybe, if it was a cow, it had brushed up against the tree and broken the branches off, though that seemed unlikely. Since they'd been stripped of their frozen crabapples I figured it had been hungry.

I wondered if maybe it hadn't been a bear, even though they're typically in hibernation that time of year. Bears don't actually hibernate, even though people think they do. It's not a true state of hibernation, but more what biologists call torpor, and bears will sometimes wake up during the winter and move around and sometimes even go out of their den, even though they're not usually very awake, then eventually go back in. Maybe they're checking to see if it's spring. But if this bear had come out of hibernation, it certainly was wide awake, because it had been able to tear up that tree and make a bed under it, using the branches.

It was still too cold outside to really do anything, and when I tried to get the dogs out for their walk they didn't even want to go out the door, so I decided to stay inside and do some baking. I'm not the world's greatest cook, but when it's cold like that I enjoy puttering around in the kitchen.

So, I started off making a big batch of chocolate chip cookies, Chrissie's favorite. After I got those in the oven, I started a big crockpot stew. It would take most of the day to cook but would make a delicious dinner.

I called Janie and told her to send Chrissie over for some cookies. Because our houses are next door to each other except for the big lawn between, we'd let Chrissie walk down the alleyway from one house to the other, as long as one of us kept an eye on her.

So, here she came, all excited for cookies, and as I gave her a big plate and was sending her back on her way, she said, "Grammy, the Cookie Monster came back last night."

OK, I have to say I was even more concerned now, given what I'd seen in the yard. She then added, "But Grammy, you'll be glad to know I didn't open the window for him, even though he wanted me to."

I asked, "Chrissie, how can you hear him talking when he's outside?"

She replied, "Grammy, I can't really hear him talking, but I can tell what he wants me to do. It's kind of like when you can barely hear something, kind of fuzzy."

Well, that upset me even more, though I was beginning to think she'd imagined it all. But I did walk her home that evening instead of letting her go by herself.

That night was quiet. By morning, the cold spell still hadn't broken, and as I filled the birdfeeders, I looked at the burn scars up on the hillside and once again saw something dark up there.

I went back inside and got my binoculars, standing inside the house by the big door, watching. Whatever it was, it was large, dark, and moved very little. I couldn't really get a good look at it, and I again thought it was probably a deer trying to stay warm, though it was odd, because they usually avoided the burn scars like the plague. I think they could sense that the ground wasn't stable. The thought had occurred to me more than once that the whole hillside could eventually subside and come crashing down on top of all the houses.

That night, things got pretty tense. I had just gone to bed when I got a phone call from Janie telling me that Chrissie was beside herself and wanting me to come over. Apparently she was scared to death of something, though my daughter couldn't figure out what it could possibly be.

By then it was pitch dark, and I had to admit that I was kind of nervous about going over there—I had an odd sense that something wasn't right. Was Chrissie picking up on the same feeling, or was I just echoing her fears? I knew kids could be really sensitive to environmental noises, as their lack of life experience made them less able to explain things, and their imaginations could run wild.

I put on my coat and headed for Chrissie's with my big flashlight, and even though their house was nearby, I pretty much ran as fast as I could. When I got there, Chrissie hugged me, crying. I got down beside her and asked her what was wrong, and she said the Cookie Monster had been back and was telling her to come outside, and she didn't want to go outside. It had then told her to open the door and slip outside when her mom wasn't looking, because it had something for her. She knew this wasn't right, and yet she loved the Cookie Monster, so she was conflicted and scared.

Janie just looked puzzled, so I told her what I'd seen up by the burn scars. We started talking, which may not have been a good idea, considering Chrissie was listening to us.

Well, now we were all nervous, and Janie asked if I would spend the night. I agreed and went back to get the dogs, once again feeling extremely vulnerable as I ran down the alley, even more so than before.

Now, my dogs are good little dogs and would usually walk right beside me without leashes, especially going over to my daughter's, because we did this all the time, but they didn't want to go outside. I had to get their leashes and pretty much force them to come with me, which I found odd.

In retrospect, I can look back at all these red flags and see that together they told a story, but at the time, I wasn't receptive to the fact that something was happening, as I was trying to fit things into a logical framework I was familiar with.

Well, I got back over to my daughter's and got settled in, sleeping with Chrissie so she wouldn't be so scared. Janie sometimes sleeps with her when her husband's gone, but that particular night Chrissie wanted me there. I don't know why, but I suspect it was because she thought I knew how to deal with the Cookie Monster.

I made sure the window was locked and the curtains closed, then climbed into Chrissie's bed with her, the dogs sleeping on a blanket I'd put on the floor for them. There was barely enough room for me and Chrissie in the bed, especially since she was such a wild sleeper, wiggling and moving around. Sometimes, when she spent the night at my house, I'd wake up to find her feet in my face, as she'd manage to turn all the way upside-down in her sleep.

But that night she was as calm as I'd ever seen her, kind of clinging to me, and I knew she felt very uneasy. I put my arm around her and sang to her and rocked her until she went to sleep, then I, too, finally drifted off.

Sometime during the night I woke, Chrissie tugging on my arm. She whispered, "Grammy, the Cookie Monster's here. He wants me to come outside."

I told her to be real still. I listened, but heard nothing. I was still half-thinking it was her imagination, which, combined with the possible cow in the yard, was making us all edgy. And if there really was something out there, surely the dogs would alert me, and yet they were sleeping. I reached down by the bed to pet Shoots, as he always slept as close to me as possible, but he wasn't there!

I turned on the little night light, only to see the dogs were gone! I called them, and they came out from under the bed, where they'd been hiding, then hurriedly went right back under.

Something had to be scaring them, but I hadn't heard a thing. Now Chrissie started crying, saying the Cookie Monster had something special for her, and he really wanted her to come outside and get it. I told her I was taking her into her mom's room, then I'd go outside to see what the Cookie Monster had for her, but she was to stay with her mom, no matter what.

Well, Janie was already awake as she'd heard us talking. Chrissie crawled into bed with her, and I put on my shoes and coat and got a flashlight. There was no way I was actually going outside to look around, but I would stick my head out the door and shine the light around and see what I could see. Whatever it was, maybe it would leave once it saw the light.

I slowly opened the back door, careful to not let the dogs out, then realized they were still hiding under the bed. Normally, they'd be the first to want to get involved in whatever was going on, but not this time.

As I slowly stuck my head around the corner of the house, I heard the sound of something big running across the yard. Shining my light, I could see a huge upright figure quickly disappear around the side of my house!

Were we dealing with a human? If so, it had to be someone huge and who looked like they were wearing a thick fur coat. I ducked back into Janie's house, scared and confused.

Chrissie slept with her mom for the rest of the night, and I slept on the couch, the dogs finally coming out from beneath the bed and trying to pile onto it with me. I say slept, but in reality, I tossed and turned all night.

The next morning, as soon as there was enough light, I went out into the yard and looked for tracks. The snow was all smashed down near Chrissie's window, which gave me pause, confirming there had indeed been something there. I couldn't make out any individual tracks, just a lot of trampled snow.

After we all had breakfast, I took the dogs and headed back over to my house, where I found the back door open and the house freezing inside. I was able to pull the door shut, even though it was off one of its hinges, and I then cranked up the heat, hoping my pipes hadn't frozen.

I was nervous to walk through the house, afraid that whoever had broken in might still be there. The dogs were running around sniffing everything excitedly. When I walked into the kitchen, I could see my crockpot was gone, stew and all!

Had someone kicked in my door just to steal my crockpot? It seemed surreal. I had a number of valuable things right in plain sight —my TV, stereo, computer—and all they'd taken was my stew? I was incredulous.

I was now pretty certain we were dealing with a bear, and this seemed even more obvious when I saw the empty crockpot out in the yard. But why would Chrissie keep saying it was talking to her, trying to entice her to go outside?

It wasn't long before Janie called me. She'd been checking the community Internet page and a six-year-old boy had gone missing during the night. His parents said he'd just disappeared, and since they always locked their house, it looked like he'd run away, as no one had broken in. They were desperately looking for him and had put out the call for people to be alert, and the police were also involved.

When Janie said the boy lived less than a block from us, I knew he'd somehow gone with Chrissie's Cookie Monster. I felt sick, knowing it could've easily been Chrissie.

Well, fortunately my pipes weren't frozen, and I called a repairman to fix the door. As he worked, I again took out my binoculars and looked at the burn scars on the hillside above the house.

The dark figure was there! I watched it for the longest time, but it didn't move. It must be sleeping, I figured, after a long night. But where was the boy? I was almost certain this guy or bear or whatever it was had taken him.

I suddenly saw movement below the burn scars—a deer or something was slowly walking down the mountainside. I focused on it, only to find it looked like a child! It was trying to make its way downwards through the thick brush! I called the repairman over and he took a look, then agreed it had to be a child.

I was soon on the phone with the sheriff, and it didn't take long for them to get there, quickly climbing the hillside. I again looked up at the burn scars, but the figure was gone.

I watched as they found the child, and it wasn't long before a deputy stopped by my house to talk to me, since I'd been the one to call it in. Sure enough, it was the missing boy, and other than being scared to death, he was fine. They would interview him in more detail later, but for now, he'd simply told them that he'd gone hiking with a big hairy man, and they'd spent the night near the warmth of the burning coal seam.

I spent a good deal of time talking to this deputy, and I told him all about Chrissie and how my house had been broken into. I also told him how I'd seen someone up at the burn scars. He recorded our interview, then told me he was going to get some of his guys to go up and check things out.

Not long afterwards, I watched through my binoculars as several men climbed the mountainside, slowly making their way through the thick scrub oak and snow. I would occasionally scan back up to the burn scars, but saw nothing.

They eventually got to the scars, and I could see them looking around, and it wasn't long before they made their way back down. I knew they hadn't found anyone.

Later, the sheriff called to update me on what they'd found. First, lots of tracks in the mud around the burn scars, but he wouldn't say much about what kind of tracks, kind of dodging my questions. But more importantly, he said one of the burn areas was caved in, and all that remained was a deep dark hole. He was going to contact the state and get them to come out and reclaim it or whatever they do, fencing it in or closing up the hole so it wasn't a danger to anyone.

When I said I was happy the young boy hadn't fallen in, the sheriff said he'd talked to him, and there wasn't a hole when the boy was up there. This particular burn area was where the boy had been with the so-called big hairy man, which I knew had to be Chrissie's Cookie Monster.

Things settled down after a few days, and I never saw anything up at the burn scars again, though I did look frequently, still unsettled by it all. I eventually told my daughter and her husband I was moving.

I needed to be able to see out, and sitting in my living room and seeing the Burning Mountain reminded me of the terror I'd felt. My mental health was starting to be affected, and I'd even started having nightmares about falling into a deep hole. I was actually hoping I could talk them into moving, too. Janie could get a nursing job anywhere, and Eric could also work from almost anywhere, being a truck driver.

Shortly after making my decision, I had a strange dream. In my dream I could hear a voice say, "Come outside." I got up and went to the window, and pulling back the curtains, I saw a creature that did indeed look like the Cookie Monster, except with a flat nose and big square teeth. It reminded me of a gorilla, except it seemed human-like. It turned and walked away. I crawled back into bed like someone in a trance and tried to sleep, tossing and turning all night.

The next morning, it seemed real, but I knew it had been a dream. I recalled when one of my dogs had died a couple of years before. She was really old and passed in her sleep one night. I was distraught, and a few nights later I woke up, knowing she was at the back door, wanting in. I got up and went to the door, and sure enough, there she stood. I let her in and went back to bed. Of course, the next morning she wasn't there, and I knew it had been a dream, yet it had felt so real.

This felt the same way. But even though I knew it was a dream, I started packing my stuff.

Janie and Chrissie came over later, bringing some soup for dinner, and it was all I could do to not cry, as I knew I would miss them terribly. As we were eating, Chrissie said, "Grammy, the Cookie Monster came last night, but I told him to go away. I don't want him around anymore."

Janie and I looked at each other with alarm. I now knew we all had to get out of there, that my dream had been real, and this thing hadn't fallen into the hole on the mountain. But there was no way I could leave without convincing them to go, too.

That night, even though I was still fatigued from not getting enough rest the night before, I couldn't sleep. How could I talk Janie and her husband into leaving? I finally got up and sat on the couch where I could see over to Janie's, noting that her living-room light was on. I eventually fell asleep.

The next day, Janie called. She'd been up all night looking for rentals on the Internet. She was obviously as worried as I was.

She said, "Mom, I had a nice long talk with Eric this morning. He's on his way home, and we've decided to move to eastern Colorado, out on the prairie, where Eric's mom lives. She has a nice farm there, and we're going to put a modular on her place. Eric can work from anywhere, and I might be able to be a full-time mom, as things there are so much cheaper, plus we won't have rent."

I felt a deep sadness come over me, a feeling that I was about to lose everything, even though mere hours before I'd been prepared to move away myself. But this was different—I guess I'd harbored hopes that Janie and Chrissie would move near to wherever I decided to go.

But Janie wasn't done. "And we want you to come, too. The old farmhouse is way too big for one person, and Eric's mom said you could live in part of it. You could help with Chrissie whenever you wanted and we'd still get to see you, but you could also travel when you want to get away."

I was ecstatic! If I didn't have to pay much rent, I could actually afford to travel some, which I enjoyed.

Well, we all finally got moved, and I have to say that I've really grown to like it there, as the views are wonderful, though at first I thought there wasn't much to see except endless fields. I've grown to love the sight of distant storms moving across the prairie, and I'm getting more familiar with the all the kind of birds.

Anyway, it's been a lot of fun fishing here with you, Rusty. I keep saying I'm going to climb up to the burn scar on the mountain while I'm here and look at that hole, but to be honest, the very thought gives me the willies. I don't know what happened to that creature thing, but there were no more reports after we left, so maybe it left, too.

I don't know, maybe both me and Chrissie were dreaming that night we thought it came back, and it really did fall into that hole. All I can say is I'm glad we now live where it won't come visit us, or at least so I hope.

4

TERROR IN THE BLACK CANYON

Gabby and I met while I was fishing the beautiful Roaring Fork River near Glenwood Springs, Colorado. I was just enjoying the fishing for once, no clients to tend to, testing out the famous Gold Medal catch and release waters there.

I wondered if maybe I wasn't fishing in the wrong place or something when she pulled up near the shore and got out of a white pickup with the words "Colorado Parks and Wildlife" on its side. But she said hello and asked me what was biting, then said she was there to do a fish survey.

It's not often I get to talk to a fish biologist, so we ended up spending quite some time talking, which eventually segued into the following story. I found it to be astounding, even though I've heard some pretty incredible Bigfoot tales. Maybe it was the telling of it, but I think it also had to do with the setting in which it took place, the deep and mysterious Black Canyon of the Gunnison. —Rusty

I'm pretty hesitant to tell you about this incident, Rusty, but I guess if you don't believe me you won't be the first. After it happened, I felt the need to talk to people about it, but I soon found that most everyone thought I was either making it up or was mentally unbalanced, or maybe both. In any case, I've gotten to where I don't really care what people think, because I know the truth, but I rarely talk about it anymore. But given that you seem open to hearing my story, here goes.

Let me preface what I'm going to tell you by saying that most of us live in a world that doesn't include big hairy monsters. We're pretty ignorant of what's actually out there, and maybe that's a good thing, for if people knew, they would never go outdoors.

I do believe nature can be healing and good for us, as long as you watch where you're going. It's probably a good idea to stay away from places where Bigfoot might be found, though how would you know? A lot of people say Bigfoot is harmless, and maybe it's true, but the one I saw seemed to have an agenda, and that agenda included getting rid of me. But who knows—maybe it was just trying to intimidate me so I would leave, which worked.

My experience left me traumatized, the exact opposite of how I usually feel when out in the natural world. As a result, something valuable and special has been taken from me, and now I'm always on edge when I go out in certain places alone, though I have no choice because of the nature of my work.

Going out in the woods is part of my job. I'm a fish biologist for Colorado Parks and Wildlife, which means I study the behavior of fish in their natural surroundings, as well as count them and check for disease and such. I need to be comfortable in nature, which I generally am, though I refuse to go back to the place where my encounter happened.

I use the word encounter for lack of anything better, but it sure doesn't capture what I felt, as it was more than just an encounter, it was a full-on assault. The wildlife department let me transfer to a new area afterwards, here along the Roaring Fork and other nearby waterways, but they never knew why I wanted to move. Who in their right mind would tell their boss a Bigfoot had been after them? You'd probably get fired or at the very least, recommended for therapy.

Where was I when this happened? Well, I was way down in the bottom of the Black Canyon of the Gunnison in Western Colorado, doing a fish survey on the Gunnison River. I routinely conducted surveys there, as that river section has around 9,000 fish per mile, which is the highest concentration of fish on that particular river. It was always exciting to see all the huge rainbow and brown trout there. It's a section designated as Gold Medal and Wild Trout Water, though you have to be pretty dedicated to get down to it, as the river's in the bottom of the steep canyon.

Every time I did a survey, I had to steel myself for the trip, for getting into the canyon was a job in itself, as was getting back out.

A lot of people have never heard of the Black Canyon, as it's Colorado's least-visited national park. It's called that because it's so deep that the sunlight is filtered by the shadows, making it look dark and mysterious. It also has some of the oldest rock in the world, a dark Precambrian schist that adds to the mesmerizing depths. And, to top it off, it has the highest cliff in Colorado, the Painted Wall, which is 2,250 feet tall. It's really stunning with bands of pink granite slashing through the dark metamorphic rock.

Well, I always kind of dreaded when I had to go down there, because it was physically really hard. It was kind of like the opposite of mountain climbing, a steep 2,000-foot drop from the rim to the river. I'd go down the trail by Gunnison Point, a precipitous drop down slopes covered in loose dirt, rock, and big boulders. It was so steep in places that I'd have to go down on my rear end, and sometimes I'd just toss my pack and let it roll on down the slope, saving me having to carry it, though it would kind of beat it up. I also carried a small inflatable kayak, which I would sometimes need to get out on the river.

Once on the bottom, there were a number of nice places to pitch my little tent, assuming there weren't any fishermen already camping there. The ones who did go were kind of purists, and I think they went more for the experience than the fishing, though I seldom saw anyone. It's nice and quiet, like a primeval world. The one thing you really have to watch out for is poison ivy, which grows everywhere along the river. It thrives in sunless, wet areas, which the Black Canyon is famous for.

But there is another thing you have to look out for, which I'll get to shortly.

It's an intimidating place, actually, very intense and foreboding. The canyon itself is around 14 miles long, but you can't hike it because the river goes right up to the cliffs in a number of places, and at one point, the water even disappears under the rocks for a ways. It has been kayaked, but you better know what you're doing, as there are a number of really terrifying waterfalls and places you have to portage around, like where it disappears.

Typically, I'd make my way down the steep canyon wall, then find a nice place at the bottom by the river under the cottonwoods and box elders, then set up my little tent and make camp. I'd usually spend at least one or two nights, as it's such an effort getting in and out that doing it in one day didn't leave time to do any work.

Once all set up, I'd start work by mid-afternoon, netting fish and checking them over for various diseases, as well as counting them. By late afternoon, I'd be pretty tired and would call it a day, having a sandwich and granola for dinner. I never carried a stove, as it just added to the weight, and eating cold food for a couple of days didn't bother me.

Later, after my experience, I read a lot about Bigfoot, and some say the smell of cooking food draws them in, but I knew that wasn't true in my case. I'm not sure what actually brought the thing down the canyon, nor why it was so angry.

It was late August and my last trip into the canyon, though I didn't know it at the time. The river was low, a good time to check fish, as I could pretty much wade out as far as I needed to go. In fact, I was wondering why I'd bothered to bring my kayak, as it seemed like extra weight and bulk, but I went ahead and blew it up and left it by my tent. I was later very glad for that.

It was hot when I'd left the rim, but as I sat on a log in front of my tent eating my cold dinner, I felt a chill come over everything as a breeze came down the canyon, which has its own microclimate, sunlight lighting the river for only a few minutes at midday.

I knew it was still early, maybe all of four o'clock, though it already felt like dusk. The days are short in the canyon, which in some places is deeper than it is wide. It wasn't yet autumn, but I could see and feel it coming with the chilly air and yellow leaves on the box elders, and it made me feel poignant.

The canyon was empty, no one there but me, and I felt a sudden sense of loneliness, something I rarely felt. All was still, and even the river sounded subdued, its low water a far cry from the roar of early snowmelt that one could hear clear from the rim in the spring. It seemed almost sad, like it would soon be locked in the icy grip of winter.

As the shadows grew deeper, I slipped into my longjohns and got ready for bed, even though it was still early. I knew the sheer walls of dark gray stone above me provided refuge for peregrine falcons and golden eagles, but all I saw were a few swallows swooping above the water, eating insects.

Everything seemed somber and almost deathly, and I began to wonder if I'd somehow gotten off track and was imagining things. Had the canyon felt like this any of the number of times I'd been there before? I thought back, but couldn't recall feeling like this—not there or anywhere else, for that matter.

Now the darkness seemed to actually thicken, and I watched as a ribbon of starlight began to appear like a belt delineating the canyon's boundaries far above. It was a stunning sight, one I'd seen many times, but for some reason it now made me feel like I was in a giant coffin, the lid ready to be closed by some giant hand.

I shook my head, trying to clear my mind. What was going on? I finally crawled into my little tent, deciding I was tired and just needed to rest. As I began to drift off to the murmur of the river, I suddenly remembered it was my sister's birthday.

How could I forget Lucy's birthday? I chided myself. She'd been three years older than me and had been my champion, my mentor, the one who told me I could do about anything I set my mind to. She'd been tragically killed in a motorcycle accident just the year before, and I still missed her terribly.

As I lay there in my sleeping bag, I decided that was why I was having such a hard time—it was Lucy's birthday. Even though I hadn't remembered it on a conscious level, I must be thinking of her subconsciously, and it had shaded my entire day, making everything feel somber.

I cried for a bit, thinking of her, then began to drift off, tired after the long haul down into the canyon. Tomorrow would be a new day, I'd get lots done and then drag myself back up the 2,000-foot slope to where my car was parked and go home. Who knows, maybe I'd talk to my boss and see if they could get someone else to start covering the Black Canyon, though I knew this would be my last trip in for the season. Heck, maybe I should go back to school and change careers. I'd always thought it would be interesting to study wolves.

Strangely enough, the last thing I recall before drifting off was a howl, far away, and I decided it must be a coyote. I was soon fast asleep, the canyon depths haunting my dreams.

I don't know what it time it was when I heard someone talking, just outside my tent, but it felt like early morning, maybe around 4 a.m. At first I thought I was dreaming, but after a few moments, I knew it was real.

What I couldn't figure out was how it could be Lucy—there was no way, Lucy had died a year ago. I was wide awake, and yet I could hear her just outside my tent door, and she sounded disturbed.

"Gabby, get up! Get your kayak in the river. Hurry!"

Why would Lucy be there, and why would she tell me to do something so disastrous? I wasn't all that far from a set of deadly rapids that had eaten more than one kayak, and that with expert kayakers aboard. It seemed that every summer a few brave or even suicidal kayakers would try to run the Black Canyon, some not coming back out of the canyon alive. There was no way I was getting in the water, especially in the dark. Messing around with fish in calm water was one thing, but the rapids of the Black Canyon were something to be respected and feared.

Now I knew I was dreaming, having one of those waking nightmares where you think you're awake but you're not. I'd read about them, and it seemed you can't move even if you want to, so there was no danger of me putting my kayak in the water.

Everything seemed surreal, but I relaxed, now knowing I would eventually wake. But soon things got weirder—I could hear that same howling in the distance, and it seemed to be coming closer. I was suddenly hit with a visceral feeling of doom, a feeling that I was soon going to be like Lucy, gone from this world.

Lucy said, "Gabby, get up now! You're in grave danger!"

I replied, "Lucy, how can I be talking to you when you're gone? I know I'm dreaming."

"Get up and get on the river. That thing is coming for you. Get up, Gabby, please!"

"I'll drown, Lucy. I can't go down the Gunnison in the dark. I can't even do it in the daylight!"

"Just go across the river, then it won't know where you are. Wait it out, then cross back over when it's daylight and get out of the canyon. You're running out of time, go, now!"

I still thought I was dreaming, but that howl—it echoed off the canyon walls, all up and down, and it was like nothing I'd ever heard. I was quickly up, slipping into my boots and waterproof jacket, then having the presence of mind to stuff my car keys and cell phone into my pockets. I always brought my phone along, even though there was no cell service down there. I grabbed my kayak and paddle and dragged them down to the river's edge.

As I hesitated, still thinking it was all a dream, the howl started up again, loud enough to make my ears buzz. I jumped into the little kayak and pushed it out into the black water, not sure if I was more terrified of the howl or of the thought of putting into the river in the dark.

I'll add this here—to this day, I don't know if I actually heard Lucy or not. I'm not much of one for spooky kind of stuff, but something woke me with a sense of life or death urgency. Maybe it was my subconscious, knowing I would pay more attention if I thought it was my sister warning me, I don't know. But something woke me—or maybe it was the howling—but something told me I was in danger and then told me exactly what I should do. I'll never know what it was.

In any case, putting into the river in the dark was one of the scariest things I've ever done, but it wasn't nearly as terrifying as wondering what was coming down the canyon. I knew I had to get out of there, and the river was my only escape. The Gunnison is always cold, and the rocks along the shore are often moss encrusted and very slick. I knew that many had been swept to their death in the river.

But there was no way I could climb out of the canyon in the dark, and whatever it was could easily follow me. At that point, the howling was so loud that I knew it was flee or die, there was no question in my mind, dreaming or not.

I was soon caught up in the current. As I mentioned before, the river was low, but there was still enough force to immediately push me downstream. I paddled as hard as I could until I managed to push to the other side of the river.

There, sitting in a small eddy, I listened and waited in the darkness. The howling had stopped, but I could soon hear the sound of scuffling and grunting over at my camp, and I figured whatever it was had destroyed my tent and gear.

After that, all was quiet for a brief time, and I thought that whatever it was had probably moved on. I still had no idea what it could possibly be. I knew now it wasn't a coyote, and there were no wolves in that part of the country, so I was mystified, plus no wolf could ever howl that loud and long.

I sat there in the dark, the water quietly lapping against my kayak, wondering if I hadn't lost my mind. By then I knew I had to be awake, as there was no way a dream could be this real.

I'd almost decided to paddle back across and try to climb out when I realized how foolish an idea that was. Hadn't I just heard my camp being ripped up? Why would I think of going back over there? Besides, I had no idea what I was dealing with. I was totally mystified as to what I'd heard. I'd seen no one else that entire day, and humans can't howl like that.

It seemed like the longest time, but it was maybe 10 minutes later that I heard a loud nearby splash. It seemed as if someone had thrown a large rock that had landed near my kayak. I tried to figure out which direction it had come from, but it was impossible to tell.

I knew then that whatever or whoever it was had crossed the river. They had to be on my side.

As I paddled a bit, maintaining my place in the eddy, another rock came lobbing in, this one nearly hitting me with a big splash. I now panicked. Lucy was right. Something malevolent was trying to kill me.

I still had no idea if it was on my side of the river or not, but when I saw a huge shadow blocking the stars, I knew it was not only on the same side, but was now towering above me. I couldn't make out what it looked like, except it was large and very black. But what I'll remember forever is two large shining red eyes, eyes that looked like hot fire, angry and disturbed.

I immediately pushed off with my paddle, hard and straight, heading for the middle of the river where the current was strongest. I had no hesitation, for staying was now more terrifying than going down the river.

I wasn't a moment too soon, for I heard a loud splash right where my kayak had been, and I knew this thing had thrown another large rock. If I hadn't pushed off at that very second, it would've struck me dead on.

Quickly caught up in the current, I was unable to see anything, yet alone where I was going. And as my little inflatable kayak started down the river, I again heard that incredible howl just behind me, and I knew it was that creature, and it was looking for me.

I shivered, now at the complete mercy of the river, knowing I would soon be pummeled against one of the many large boulders along the canyon walls. One nice thing about my little kayak was that, because it was inflatable, it was very lightweight and easily carried by the river along the main current, kind of like a leaf. The flip side to this was that it could easily be punctured if it hit a sharp rock, and that would be the end of my ride.

Even though the river was low and I wasn't going real fast, I knew the odds were high of careening against one of the many rocks lining the banks. And just then, kabam, I hit a large rock. I gritted my teeth, expecting the little craft to start sinking, but it just bounced off and around, then was quickly back in the current, though a bit tipped.

The kayak righted itself, and it seemed we were suddenly going much faster, and I could soon hear the sound of whitewater in the distance and knew we were coming to one of the many dangerous rapids in the canyon, many which are rated Class 4. I could barely navigate the small craft in a riffle, yet alone across rapids, and the feeling of doom caught up with me right then and there.

I had to get off the river! I desperately paddled against the current, trying to slow down, then managed to get to the river's edge, plowing directly into a small stand of poison ivy. I ducked, then stepped out onto what seemed to be a sandy beach maybe all of 30 feet long.

Dragging the kayak out of the river, I realized I could now barely see my surroundings. Dawn was breaking, and I was still alive, though wet and bedraggled, my cotton longjohns now heavy with cold water. I tried to wring them out while still in them, water dripping into the sand, glad I'd had the presence of mind to put on my waterproof jacket, which was keeping the upper part of me warm.

I stood for awhile, looking back, wondering what had become of the giant creature that howled like a wolf. I then looked up at the seemingly impenetrable walls above. If I could just climb out, I knew I could find someone along the North Rim who would help, even though it was much less visited than the South Rim, where I'd come down. There was even a ranger station up there somewhere.

I knew there were several routes down to the river from the North Rim, the best-known being the S.O.B. Trail, which was used by climbers to access the Painted Wall. If I recalled correctly, there were two other routes, one being Long Draw and the other being Slide Draw, though I didn't have any idea where either was located.

Chilled, I watched as the shadows began to lift. It had been the strangest night. Had I really heard Lucy's voice? Had I really heard the strange howling and had rocks thrown at me? Was I still dreaming? As I stood there, realizing it had to be real, I started shivering, and I knew the danger wasn't over yet, for I could again hear the howling, and it wasn't that far up the river.

"Lucy," I said in a low voice, as if the creature might hear me over the sound of the river. "Lucy, what should I do now? I can't go down the river, and I can't climb out. I have nowhere to go."

And again, I heard the howling, and it sounded even closer. The river was low enough that it could easily follow me, half-walking and half-swimming, and it wouldn't be all that long before it got here.

I again felt panicked. What was going on? Why had this thing come from nowhere after me? What did I do to make it so angry it apparently wanted to kill me? I was already chilled from the water, but the howl brought a different kind of chill, as if my blood itself was cold.

Again the howling, and again and again, and it was now close, just beyond the bend in the river upstream. I had to do something! Above where I stood was a steep draw, the source of the sand that had washed down over time and formed the small beach. It looked impassible.

Again the howl, and it sounded so close! I had no choice but to go up, and if I got stranded on some cliff, so be it. There was no way I could go down the river, and climbing at least gave me a chance, better than just passively waiting to be killed.

It was then that I saw it! A human track! And more tracks, and they appeared to have come down the draw! Maybe someone had stopped here like I had and tried to make their way out, or maybe, just maybe, someone had come down from the rim!

I quickly pushed my kayak out into the water, hoping the creature would see it and follow, thinking it was me. I then hid behind a huge rock and watched.

And what I saw was beyond anything I could imagine, though I'm sure the dim light of the dawn made it seem even stranger than the reality. It was huge—a mass of muscle held together by a dark furry coat. It carried a rock as it ran through the water.

The kayak had caught its eye, and it upped its pace following after it, not seeing me. It was soon around another bend, and I immediately stepped out from behind the rock and started upwards. If it managed to catch up with the raft, it would know I'd tricked it and would backtrack, looking for me. It was now light enough that it could surely see my tracks if it did come back.

I was soon climbing a steep and nearly vertical slab of rock at the bottom of the draw, with no way around it. As I hoisted myself up, glad I was in decent shape, the thought occurred to me that this couldn't be the way out, not with this bad start.

Again, I felt doomed. Maybe, if I was lucky, I could at least get close enough to the rim that someone might hear me yelling, assuming anyone was around.

Later, after all was said and done, I read about this route on the national park website. It's called Slide Draw.

> This route is extremely steep and potentially dangerous due to loose rock and poor footing. A 30-foot nearly vertical scramble is required to start the route. It ends at the overview called the Kneeling Camel View, is one mile long with a vertical drop of 1,620 feet and has an abundance of loose rocks with pygmy rattlesnakes, bark scorpions, and poison ivy. It's not the kind of trail one chooses for an afternoon stroll, as there's actually no trail at all, just an iffy route up a steep rocky draw.

In retrospect, having climbed it, that wording was quite accurate, though I would've preferred not being able to verify their description.

Anyway, I finally managed to make it up that first steep pitch, and from there on out, it was mostly just climbing up endless rocks that constantly made you feel like you were about to lose your footing and go sliding down back to where you started, thus its name, Slide Draw.

Since it was August, it got hotter and hotter as the morning progressed. There really was no trail, I just climbed my way up slippery scree slopes and over and around huge boulders, until I began to wonder if I would make it out, having no water. Later, the park ranger I met at the rim and who gave me a ride said it usually takes most people four to five hours to climb out, but I think I did it in about two.

There's nothing like a sense of danger to motivate one to push beyond what you think you can do, and my muscles ached for days afterwards. And the entire time I was climbing out, I imagined the hot breath of that creature on my neck, though the last I saw was it following my kayak down the river. But it didn't take much to imagine it backtracking and following me out of the canyon, though I knew it could climb much faster than I ever could and would have quickly caught up with me.

After I was about two-thirds up, I took a break at the top of a scree field, gasping for air, my leg muscles starting to cramp up. I suddenly could hear the sound of rocks and trees crashing below me, and I knew the thing was following me.

I was horrified. I again heard Lucy's voice: "Start a rockslide, Gabby."

Just below me was a large rock, and I doubted I could move it, but I began pushing on it with my legs, bracing myself against a small juniper tree that barely hung by its roots. To my surprise, the rock began sliding, taking the loose rocks around it down with it. I nearly went sliding, too, grabbing onto the tree and hoping it would hold. I didn't wait to see how big of a slide I'd started, but instead again began climbing, my lungs aching.

I could hear rocks still clattering far below as I finally reached the rim. There, I followed a short trail over to the parking area for the Kneeling Camel View and leaned against the fence, hoping someone would soon come by. I was terrified the creature was still behind me, and as I was totally dehydrated, I wasn't sure how much longer I could last.

Fortunately, like I mentioned, a ranger soon came by. He seemed somewhat shocked to see me and later told me I looked like I'd seen a ghost. Most of the rangers there knew me from my work, and he asked what was going on.

I wasn't sure what to say, for I doubted very much if he would believe my story, and it could eventually lead to problems if word got out to my manager. Who knows what they would think of their backcountry employee apparently losing her mind and climbing out the wrong side of the Black Canyon?

I guess I could just say my kayak got into the fast current and dumped me on the wrong side of the river, but that kind of incompetence would surely lead to many questions.

But as we stood by his pickup while I drank as much water as I could hold, a strange distant howl came from far down in the canyon, far far away, drifting up on the canyon breezes.

The ranger looked at me, and though I simply shrugged my shoulders, we seemed to share an unspoken knowledge.

We turned and got into his truck and headed back for the South Rim, where I would retrieve my car and head home.

I called in sick the next day, then ended up using all my vacation time, trying to regain my sense of normalcy and to forget the creature's blood-red eyes. Finally, once back at work, I put in for a transfer, which I eventually got. Because it was late in the season, I didn't have to go back into the canyon—I knew I could never go down there again.

As for Lucy, I never heard her voice again, if that was even what it was, even though I've had a few other harrowing events. I still wonder if it wasn't just my own senses telling me to flee, but I guess I'll never know.

I do know one thing—I'll never set foot in the Black Canyon of the Gunnison again.

5

THE FLY HOUSE

I met James when one of my clients tripped and wrenched his knee while we were fishing on the Snake River. We went to the nearest hospital, which was in Jackson, Wyoming, where James did a great job of fixing my client up.

While there, I invited the doctor to come fishing with my group the next day, and he accepted, saying he'd adopted the philosophy of trying out new things after his divorce.

That evening, around the campfire, James told the following story. I was kind of surprised at his honesty about his emotions, as some don't want to talk about such things, but he said it was integral to his story. We all sat spellbound, hoping to never deal with this side of Bigfoot. —Rusty

My name's James, and I'm a former full-time orthopedic surgeon. I say former because I left that life far behind me a few years ago, though I'm now practicing again, but in a much more limited and less stressful way.

There were a number of reasons I quit my practice, but they basically revolved around an incident that happened when I was staying in a house on the western side of the Tetons in the little village of Alta, Wyoming.

In case you don't know, orthopedic surgeons specialize in the musculoskeletal system. I was the guy you'd see if you needed knee or hip replacement, ACL repair, shoulder replacement—well, you get the idea.

My life began changing in a major way when my wife Laura decided she wanted a divorce. Now, being a doctor is not an easy profession, and even after you get through all the rigors and long days of medical school and your internship to where you can actually start practicing, you hope things will ease up a bit, but they sometimes get even more stressful. After a number of years of hardly ever seeing me, I think my wife finally decided things would never turn around, which was probably true.

Laura and I went to college together, and she studied to be a teacher, so she was out of college long before I was, and her teaching job made it possible for me to get through medical school. I was appreciative of that at the time and still am.

Once I started actually working as a doctor, she also worked long days as a teacher, but she got summers off and I didn't. She had hoped I could at least take some time off each summer to do some of the things that normal sane people do who don't work 60 to 80 hours a week, but I was just as busy as ever, as the season made no difference. Actually, summers for me were even busier, as that's when everyone tended to hurt themselves doing outdoors activities.

Laura knew that my being a doctor would require long hours of work and sacrifice, but I don't think she really understood just how much I would be away from home. In all honesty, I didn't either, or I might've chosen a different profession. But it was what it was, and I was a dedicated doctor. I had hoped the money would ensure a good lifestyle for both of us, and it did, but I seldom had the time to actually enjoy it, yet alone see my wife, except for coming and going.

Anyway, after a number of years of this, Laura finally got kind of used to it, or so I thought. We got along great, even though I didn't see her very much. So you can imagine how gobsmacked I was when she had me served with divorce papers.

The day I was served, I came home to find my wife gone and a note saying she would be back at some point to get her stuff, and that I was to either sell the house and split it with her or somehow make restitution, especially since she's supported me through medical school. Her divorce attorney would be in touch.

Well, I went from being a fairly secure guy, or so I thought, to being an instant emotional wreck. It was only then that I realized how much I depended on Laura for my inner stability—she was my rock, and even though I didn't get to spend much time with her, she was always there for me—until all of a sudden she wasn't.

Later, I realized there'd been lots of red flags and warning signs, and she'd even told me over and over that she was unhappy and felt our marriage was collapsing, but I guess I just refused to believe it. Besides, there really wasn't anything I could do about it—or so I thought—because my job required long hours, many of which were spent doing paperwork.

I became so distraught that I actually had trouble functioning. After a week of stumbling through my appointments and surgeries, I finally went to the hospital administrator where I worked and had a long talk about what was going on and how I needed to take some time off.

I took a leave of absence a week later. I had no idea why or where I was going or what I was doing, but I knew I needed to go somewhere to get my head back together.

I'd been so busy that I had few friends, and the ones I did have were mutual friends with my wife, and I didn't feel comfortable talking to them about what looked to be the end of my marriage. But I did have one good friend, Gary, a fellow doctor, and I had a couple of long conversations with him.

He said I needed to get away from everything and clear my head and figure out what to do. I had no idea where to go, so I asked him to book me a place that was quiet and had mountains or desert or something where I could maybe go out and hike and get away from everything.

Gary loved to travel, and he remembered a house where his wife had wanted to go a couple of years before for a short vacation, though they'd ended up booking something else. He got online and checked, and sure enough it was open, so he booked it for me.

I was living in Denver at the time, and this house was near Alta, Wyoming, on the west side of the Tetons, the opposite side from Jackson. It wasn't cheap, and it was way bigger than I needed, but the setting looked perfect.

It was an old historic log house with a big central great room with tall two-story gable windows and a wing on each side with bedrooms and bathrooms, and a nice big kitchen on the backside of the big living room. Every window had a spectacular view of either the Tetons to the east or the Big Hole Mountains to the south. Big trees lined the big expansive lawns and framed the views of the Tetons, which were so close you almost felt like you could reach out and touch them.

The house sat on 50 acres at the very edge of the Jedidiah Smith Wilderness, which made it very special, but which also made it very accessible to a creature I later suspected came from that same wilderness, which I'll get to shortly, though I'd just as soon forget it.

I was soon driving from Denver to Alta, first through Salt Lake City, then to Idaho Falls and over to Driggs, Idaho which is a small town of maybe 1500 people. I instantly liked Driggs, which was quite a contrast to Denver.

Alta's only a few miles past Driggs and is in the most beautiful setting imaginable. It's actually in Wyoming, but it's the only town in Wyoming that you can't get to from Wyoming, and that's because it's on the backside of the Tetons. After I got there, I scaled it on Google Earth and the top of the Grand Teton was only 20 miles from the log house I was renting.

I'll never forget driving up the long lane to the house between grassy lawns lined with aspen and pine trees, and then unloading my stuff into the foyer and looking out those huge two story windows. My jaw dropped, and I felt like I was in a dream.

There, in all their glory, were the Tetons! The house stood at the opening of a long valley between tall hills with thick forests, with no close neighbors. Later, that dream turned into more of a nightmare, but at the time, I was totally enthralled with the house and the views.

And so, I settled in and felt fortunate to have this refuge, happy that I was able to afford to stay there. Gary had booked it for one month. I knew it would take longer than that for me to get my life back together, but I hoped I could at least come to grips with what was going on. I hadn't seen nor talked to my wife since before I was served with divorce papers.

OK, so here I was in this really beautiful setting. The house itself was over 100 years old and had some very nice touches, but it wasn't a huge trophy house, it was more just a really nice log house that was very comfortable and had been remodeled to have this huge great room with big windows.

I couldn't decide which wing I wanted to stay in, the one with the master bedroom and bath, which was on the backside of the house, or one of the two that faced toward the front side of the house, one which had a futon and the other which had two bunkbeds. I opted for the master bedroom, which was large and comfortable. The curtains were open, and I remember looking out at the dark shadows of the trees, feeling like I was on the edge of the wildest wilderness I'd ever been around.

I unpacked, then went into the kitchen and looked around a bit. I knew I would have to do a grocery run the next day, but I was hoping there might be some basics. I really wanted a cup of hot tea, but what I found instead was some hot chocolate, so I made a cup of that instead, then went and sat in the leather recliner that faced toward the big windows towards the Tetons, then watched the most spectacular sunset.

It was soon extremely dark, as there was absolutely no light pollution, and as I looked out that big window I could make out faraway dark teal shapes that I figured must be the tops of the Tetons, as I could see where the stars began just above.

There were no curtains on these big windows, making you feel as if you were actually outside. The stars took my breath away—there were so many that were so brilliant and sparkly. I can't even describe it. But it was a sight I will never forget.

I sat there for awhile, just taking it all in, kind of having forgotten my divorce for a bit, until something flew into my hair and buzzed around, making me jump up from my chair. I turned on a light and realized it was a fly.

I brushed it off and thought nothing of it—who would think anything about a fly being in their house? It was mid to late October, the time when bugs try to get in from the cold.

I was tired, not just from the trip, but also from trying to make my last week at the hospital as productive as possible. I was actually exhausted, though I didn't realize it at the time. I finally just collapsed into bed.

The next thing I knew, it was morning, and I knew there must be a fantastic sunrise going on because the curtains had turned a kind of a pinkish ruby color. I jumped out of bed and ran into the main room where I could see the sun rising over the Tetons, clouds lit up with every shade of pink and magenta imaginable. I grabbed my camera and took photos right there in my pajamas in the great room, again marveling at how fortunate I was to be able to stay in such an incredible place.

As the sunrise faded, I decided I needed to get into town for groceries, so I got in the shower, then headed for Driggs, which was only about 6 miles away. It's kind of funny to be in Wyoming and then a couple of miles later you're in Idaho.

As I was driving into town, I had a strange feeling come over me, kind of a detachment. It was the oddest sensation, almost like I'd taken some kind of drug, kind of like I was floating, and it was strong enough that I had to pull the car over and stop. I sat there for awhile until my head cleared enough that I was able to go on into town.

Now, I'm a doctor, and I'm trained in recognizing the many things that can go wrong with the human body, and believe me there are a lot. But this seemed almost psychological rather than physical. It was definitely a physical feeling, yet it seemed like it was a form of mental detachment. I figured it was from stress.

Anyway, I made it to the grocery store, got supplied up with the basics, then went to a little espresso stand and got a strong cup of coffee and drove around town in an attempt to get a feel for the place.

It doesn't take long to drive around Driggs, and I was soon back at the house, where I unloaded the groceries and made myself some lunch, a sandwich with some chips.

That helped a lot, and I decided the detached floating feeling I had going into town was probably from low blood sugar because I hadn't eaten for some time. In fact, I hadn't been eating much at all, because when I get emotionally upset I tend to lose my appetite.

I was really tired, so I spent the rest of the afternoon just loafing, then walked around the grounds a little. I then sat in the great room for awhile, reading a book on Grand Targhee trails, Grand Targhee being the ski area near the house. I could actually see one of the runs from the great room. I was thinking that maybe I would go up there and take a hike, when another fly came buzzing in and got stuck in my hair.

I knew I needed a haircut, but I wondered why the flies were going for my hair. I didn't use a hair gel or anything like that. I got up to get a drink of water and found the kitchen windows were thick with flies.

The casement windows had lever-type cranks and no screens, so I just opened them up and let all the flies out. There hadn't been any flies there earlier, so where had they come from? I wondered if maybe they'd been up in the high windows and had just now come down. But when I went into the master bedroom and saw that the windows in there were also covered with flies, I began wondering what was going on, though I really didn't think much about it, just figuring it was the time of year. Maybe there was some kind of feedlot or something nearby.

Well, that night I went into the master bedroom and went to bed early. I was exhausted, and all I wanted to do was sleep. I'd forgotten to close the curtains, and I woke up sometime in the middle of the night, feeling edgy. I don't know any other way to describe it, as it felt like I was in some kind of low-level danger. I know that sounds odd, but that's how it felt, like maybe there was something outside.

I lay there as still as could be once I realized the curtains were still open, wondering if maybe a bear or something was watching me. I'd been talking with a local guy at the grocery store who'd told me he lived in a little town near Driggs called Tetonia and had seen grizzly bears and wolves in his backyard, right in town. He also told me that there was a pack of wolves that lived in the thick forest along the base of the mountain just behind my house, which made sense, as there are wolves in Teton National Park, and the park boundary wasn't far up the valley.

So there I was, kind of scared—well, *really* scared—thinking a grizzly might be outside, and I was too scared to even get up and close the curtains. I finally kind of rolled out of bed and walked all crouched down over to the windows and pulled the curtains shut.

I then decided to sneak into the other wing of the house and sleep in one of the other bedrooms, just in case there was something out there that had seen me. That way it wouldn't know where I was. That's how scared I was, that I would even think like that. In fact, I grabbed my keys, and it even occurred to me to maybe just get in my car and drive away.

But as I started creeping in the dark from one wing to the other, I realized I would have to cross the great room with all those huge floor to ceiling windows. I knew whatever was out there would be able to clearly see me. So, I kind of crawled into the kitchen, where I wouldn't be seen, then sat on the floor and just waited.

After being uncomfortable and cold for about an hour, I decided I had to do something different. I crawled back to the master bedroom and got back in bed. Once I was down under the covers I gradually went back to sleep.

I woke the next morning, the sun shining directly in my eyes. The sun was at an angle where it would come up over the Middle Teton, and the bedroom window looked out in that direction. I was disoriented, not sure where I was, then remembered and watched the sun slowly come up, washing out the shadows from the giant crevasses up on the mountainsides.

It suddenly dawned on me that I had closed the curtains the night before.

As I sat there in bed, I recalled clearly how I'd felt during the night, and I was positive I'd closed all the curtains. So why was one now open to where the sun was in my eyes? I finally decided I must've not closed it all the way. I was so exhausted that it was something I could've possibly done, but it left me feeling unsettled.

It was late, maybe 9 a.m., and I was hungry, so I headed for the kitchen, making myself a cup of coffee and some breakfast. I was braced to see the windows full of flies, but there was nary a one. It was a beautiful day, and after breakfast I walked around the grounds and down the lane to the main road, which led on up to the Grand Targhee ski area and to hiking trails in the Teton Valley.

There in the shadows of the mighty Tetons, the place was just beautiful, and I wondered why I'd been so edgy during the night. I finally decided it was because I wasn't used to being alone. This made me think of my wife, and an overwhelming sadness came over me. I wanted so badly to call her, but she'd blocked my calls and any other way I had to get ahold of her. I can't tell you how forlorn I felt.

I went back inside and made a cup of tea, and I basically sat in the big recliner all afternoon and evening until the sunset covered the Tetons with alpenglow, then a black darkness fell on everything, including me.

I finally got up and turned on some lights, but I once again felt uncomfortable sitting in the great room with no curtains with the inky blackness outside, the glass windows being the only thing separating me from an imaginary pack of wolves. So, I retreated to the master bedroom where I made sure the curtains were closed and even closed the bedroom door. I then crawled into bed, finally drifting off to sleep.

I woke in the middle of the night to the strangest sound, and I didn't move, trying to figure out what it was. I thought for the longest time that it was some kind of strange electrical buzzing, and I wondered if maybe I shouldn't get up and get in my car and sleep, for maybe the house's electrical system had somehow gone haywire. I even wondered if the house might burn down.

The sound was coming from the great room, and I finally got up and cracked the door a little. I couldn't see anything, but I instantly knew what it was—the sound of thousands of flies buzzing around in the dark. Now, we all know flies are quiet at night and don't generally fly around, but there were obviously flies buzzing around the great room in enough quantities that it actually woke me up.

I didn't know what to do, wondering if I hadn't maybe lost my mind. How could there be so many flies all of a sudden? Where would thousands of flies hang out during the day? The only thing I could come up with was they were way up high in the peak of the two-story room—but it just didn't make sense.

I finally went back to sleep, as there was nothing else I could do. When I got up the next morning, I carefully opened the bedroom door, but I didn't see any flies buzzing around. But sure enough, the kitchen windows were filled with them, so I again let them out.

Were they going out during the day and then somehow finding their way through some hole in the chinking and coming back in at night for the warmth? It was a puzzler, and it was beginning to detract seriously from my enjoyment of the house. And what didn't help was seeing a card for an exterminator in a basket in the kitchen. Obviously the problem wasn't new.

As I again sat in the recliner drinking coffee and watching the sunrise over the Tetons, it dawned on me that my time was passing quickly, and I had no idea where I would go next. Other than the flies, I was starting to kind of like the house and the feeling of being on the edge of wilderness, though at night it was unsettling and felt too primal. I wanted to go out and look at the stars, but I was too afraid, picturing wolves hanging out by the door with grizzly bears and mountain lions, waiting for me.

So, as the days went on, I gradually got a little more used to living right at the edge of the wildlands, in the last house before the huge Jedediah Smith Wilderness. During the day, looking out at the thick forest and steep mountain ramparts filled me with a sense of awe, but at night, it gave me a feeling of trepidation and even fear. I remember going through all the drawers everywhere looking for bear spray, though I never found any.

I guess I must've been getting rested up, because I decided to drive on into town again and look around some more. I drove to a wetlands just past Driggs where moose supposedly hung out, and sure enough, I did see several. One had a huge rack, and I tried to get a picture of it, but it was too far off. I then drove on over to the other side of the valley towards the Big Hole Mountains, then to the small town of Victor.

It was a beautiful sunny day, and I really enjoyed the drive and getting out and taking some pictures, and I stopped in Victor and got a nice takeout lunch from a deli. I then went to the park there and ate, kind of enjoying seeing people and watching the kids at the playground.

It then dawned on me that I was actively trying to stay away from the log house. The thought of going back brought on a sense of loneliness and edginess. Thinking along those lines made me stop at a small general store and buy a can of bear spray.

Well, though I felt reluctant, it was almost dark, so I headed back. When I got there, I turned on all the lights and felt a little more comfortable in the great room, curtains or not. I started looking through the magazines on the coffee table and found a small book I hadn't noticed before.

I opened it, realizing it was a guest register, and started reading some of the entries, most of which were pretty typical, things like, we had a great time, beautiful views, will be back, that kind of thing. But as I kept reading, one entry really struck me. It said, "Thank you for letting us use your beautiful house in the most beautiful setting. My family and I come back to the Fly House every year and will be back again next year."

The Fly House. That really struck me. So, the flies weren't

anything new. I opened the book again and looked at the date the note had been written, and seeing it was in June, I was puzzled, because flies just don't come inside like that except in the autumn.

Somehow, the house was a refuge for flies. I didn't really see that many around during the day except on the kitchen windows, which I would open, and that would be it for the day, although I occasionally would see one or two here and there. But the Fly House—what a strange thing to call someone's resort rental.

I turned on the television, thinking I'd find something to watch, but I've never been a big TV watcher, so that didn't last long. Besides, I was beginning to feel unsettled and edgy again, and I wondered if it wasn't from feeling like a sitting duck in the great room with all the lights on and huge windows everywhere.

I decided to again retreat to the master bedroom, but yet it, too, was starting to feel kind of dark. I remembered again finding the curtain open, plus I just hadn't slept that well in there.

I decided to go hang out in one of the other bedrooms. The bedroom with a futon actually felt kind of secure, and I think it was because it was on the side of the house right next to the driveway. There weren't any wild areas or anything out the window, just a driveway and grassy lawn. So, I got a book and went in there and made myself comfortable.

I started feeling like it was time to go to bed, but I felt reluctant to go back to the master bedroom, so I got my pajamas and basically moved into the futon room. I slept really well that night and the edgy feeling seemed to go away, and I didn't wake up to the sound of flies buzzing.

Well, in spite of the pleasant night, the next day everything basically came crashing down. I made the mistake of trying to get ahold of Laura, even though she'd left me a letter telling me not to contact her. I just couldn't help it.

I felt that if I could just talk to her, maybe we could fix things up. Her letter had said, "You were never around to talk to me when I needed you, so don't bother trying to call me when you realize this is over. I'm really sorry, but you had lots of warnings that our marriage was failing and took no steps to do anything. Don't contact me."

I knew she'd blocked me on her email and phone, so I ended up calling her brother, Ralph. Well, Ralph and I had been friends, and he did talk to me for a little bit, but I can't say I liked what he told me. He basically said that he was sorry things had come to this, but Laura had asked him not to give me any kind of information about where she was or what she was doing.

I was pretty much dumbfounded, and I told Ralph so, asking if she thought I was going to stalk her or something. I then realized I was doing exactly what she'd asked me not to do, trying to find out where she'd gone. I told Ralph I was sorry and wouldn't bother him again.

Well, I felt numb. There's no other way to put it, except to say that my denial was now totally gone. I finally had to come to grips with what was going on—my beautiful wonderful wife had left me, and not only had she left me, but she didn't even want to be friends anymore. I figured she would probably take me to the cleaners, but I really didn't care. I'd just go be a bum and live in an old trailer or something. I had no interest in being a doctor again, though I had no idea how I was going to support myself otherwise.

To say I was distraught was an understatement. I started pacing the floor, feeling a sense of panic that my life was pretty much over. I at first thought this was all because I loved Laura, but after awhile I began to realize that to me she represented security, and I was basically like a little kid inside.

It was kind of a shock to realize how much I'd depended on her for everything. No wonder she'd left me. It wasn't an equal relationship. Sure, I'd provided her with everything she wanted, a nice house and nice vehicle, and she could travel the world, but I wouldn't be there with her because I was too busy working. I then had the sinking feeling that I had a serious problem, one that I'd hid under the guise of being a busy doctor because it worked so well, but the truth was, I was a workaholic. I used my work to hide from reality and my own emotions.

I sat in that big leather recliner for hours in the dark, and I no longer cared if something was looking at me—I just didn't care. I was beside myself and didn't know what to do or where to go.

I started crying, and I cried and cried and cried, feeling sorry for myself, then that turned into a feeling of hopelessness. At that point I begin sobbing out loud, and the sobbing turned into a wailing sound. I sounded like a wounded animal, and it gradually dawned on me that there was something outside. I couldn't see it, but I could hear it, and it sounded just like me. It was also wailing.

I can't tell you how quickly I went from total utter despair to total utter terror. Whatever it was, I could see its eyes shining, and they were up off the ground a good eight feet. It was a giant grizzly bear or something! I froze.

It had glowing red eyes, looking in at me, and I knew it could see me, even though it was dark inside. All I could think of was that I had to get out of there—right then, whatever it took, that my life was in danger. I quickly grabbed my wallet and car keys, and since my laptop was right there, I also grabbed it. I was so terrified I'm surprised I remembered anything.

I ran and jumped in my car, but it wouldn't start! The battery acted like it was half-dead, and I had no idea why, because I'd been driving around enough that it should've been well-charged. I finally got it to turn over, to my relief.

As I started down the drive, I glanced back toward the dark house and thought I could see something, a dark shadow, something big and black standing near the house. I started feeling that sense of detachment again, then I began feeling that I was being dramatic and should stay and rest and make a cup of tea. It was really strange, like the thought was coming from outside my own mind, like someone was telling me this without using words. I managed to pull myself together and get out of there.

Now shaking, I drove on into Driggs and pulled into the grocery store parking lot, where I knew I could sit, surrounded by lights and people going in and out. It felt very safe.

As I sat there, I realized I was scared to death. I didn't know what to do, and I felt like I'd lost my mind. I finally got out of the car and went inside, just wanting to be around people. I got a cart and slowly walked up and down the aisles, putting a few things in, just savoring the lights and the people and the feeling of safety.

Well, I couldn't stay in the grocery store all night, so I finally checked out and got back in my car and tried to figure out where to go. I finally went out to the edge of town where I remembered seeing a couple of motels, and I got a room. I can't tell you how nice it felt to be in a motel with other people around.

After I settled down a bit, I ate the sandwich I'd bought and kind of kicked back, watched the news, and felt like I was getting my bearings again. It had been a truly awful day. I'd never fallen apart like that in my entire life, and I've been through a number of harrowing events as a doctor. I felt totally depleted, and I needed to talk to somebody, so I called my friend Gary.

I told him there'd been something big outside the house, and I'd gotten a motel room. Well, Gary is one of the most levelheaded people you'll ever meet, and he really tried to be there for me that night. He basically talked me down, telling me I was emotionally very sensitive because of what had happened with Laura, and I would feel better tomorrow, that I should go back out to the house the next day and look for tracks, and in the meantime he would contact the owner and see if there was any way I could get out of the lease.

I slept well, even when a bunch of motorcyclists revved up in the parking lot in the middle of the night. Normally, something like that would irritate me, but when they woke me up, I felt a sense of how nice it was to be in civilization and went right back to sleep. The next morning, I got up and showered, even though I didn't have a change of clothes, but I felt much better, and I went back into town and got some breakfast.

Gary called about mid-morning. Stan, the owner of the rental, would be out around one to meet with me and walk around the house. That sounded OK, so I headed back up the hill, making sure I didn't get there until one, as I didn't feel comfortable alone.

We walked all around the house. It was hard to find anything in the grass, but we did find a couple of tracks coming in from the road to the grassy area, and they were huge, but the owner said they were bear tracks. He added that he'd had a bear come up there a few times before he'd turned it into a resort rental and moved into town, and there had never been an incident in the entire valley of a bear harming anyone, and as long as I had bear spray handy, I'd be fine.

Well, after it was all said and done and he left, I started thinking about this guy, and I figured he hadn't been straightforward with me at all. I'd actually kind of had that feeling when he was there talking to me, but because I was so out of kilter, I didn't trust my intuition.

In spite of how I felt about him, I finally decided that it had to have been a bear, so I went back inside and tried to focus on how lucky I was to be there, right under the beautiful Tetons. I would make the most of it. I talked to Gary again, and he said the owner had decided since it was just a bear that I should stay and not worry about it, and he wasn't going to refund my money. Keep in mind that this was a very expensive resort rental, and I'd paid him a lot to stay there.

I brought in the groceries I'd bought the night before and made myself some dinner, then I decided to try and enjoy the setting. I went outside and walked around the grounds, watching the birds and taking some photos of the mountains. It really was a beautiful place, and I felt irritated that this bear thing was ruining my enjoyment of it. I would stay and keep my bear spray handy.

I walked around on the grassy stretches of lawn, not getting too far from the house, still feeling uncertain, when I saw a small whitetail deer lying in the grass under some aspen trees. I tried to sneak up on it to get a good photo, and I'd nearly succeeded when it jumped up and ran off.

I was disappointed, and I walked on over to where it had been, out of curiosity. It was then that I saw what looked like a small root cellar dug into a small hill. I could tell it was really old from the rotted logs, and I figured it was part of the original homestead.

Inside was a hole wide enough to be a bear den, though I couldn't see how far back it went. It seemed mysterious and unnatural, like something had dug into the back of the root cellar, enlarging it. As I stood there, I heard a buzzing sound, and I realized the hole seemed to be home to a bunch of flies! I could hear them buzzing around inside, and every once in awhile, some would fly out.

Was this where all the flies were coming from? If so, how did they end up in the house? I suddenly felt like I was in danger, and I turned and hurried back to the house, where I fled into the security of the futon room. I would sleep there from now on.

As it started to get dark, I made sure all the doors were locked, and I turned on all the outside lights, which lit the yard up pretty good. I hadn't been doing that before, mostly because I didn't want to waste electricity. I also gathered my stuff from the master bedroom and put everything I wasn't using in my car. I wanted to be prepared, though I wasn't sure for what.

I settled into the futon room, kicking back, thinking about the root cellar and the flies, then mentally counting the days I had left there and wondering where I should go next. I actually didn't even think about Laura. In retrospect, the previous day had been kind of a peak for me emotionally—it was almost as if I was starting to accept reality, as much as I didn't like it.

Well, that night things took a turn for the worse, if possible. I went to bed and slept really well until sometime in the middle of the night, when I was again awakened by the buzzing noise. I lay there awake, listening.

So, this was the Fly House, I mused, thinking of the note in the guest book. There was something about the house that attracted and probably also bred flies, which I was beginning to find pretty distasteful, especially since a couple of them had flown into my dinner, making me toss it in the trash. I could hear them flying around out there, wherever they came from, and I had no intentions of opening my door.

And as I was starting to doze off and was almost asleep, I suddenly jolted wide awake, sensing the most cutting feeling of danger I'd ever felt in my life.

When I was an undergraduate in Colorado, I loved cross-country skiing, and one time, a friend and I were caught up in an avalanche in the mountains. I'll never forget the terror of being tumbled down the mountainside, totally helpless, knowing I was going to die, though we were lucky and managed to ride it out.

And the feeling I had that night sitting in my bed in the Fly House was even more terrifying than that avalanche. I've thought back about that night a lot, and I think it was because it was a different kind of terror, more than just fear, the kind of terror you feel when you're dealing with the unknown, with something that feels malevolent, and you don't even know what you're dealing with.

I could hear the flies buzzing in the great room, and I could then hear the sound of something very heavy walking across the floor coming towards my bedroom door. There was no lock on the door, and I knew I was a sitting duck.

My first thought was how stupid I'd been to come back and let the owner convince me all was well, when I'd known better. My second thought was how stupid I was to not listen to my intuition. My third thought was how stupid I was to worry about the money I'd spent instead of leaving immediately.

Now something was outside my door. I slipped into my shoes, then dialed 911, even though I knew it would be a good 15 or 20 minutes before anyone could possibly show up. I then remembered I had the bear spray and took off the safety, wishing I'd at least tested it and made sure I knew how to use it. I sat there on my bed, bear spray in hand, waiting for that door to open, wondering if a bear knew how to turn the knob, though something inside me said it wasn't a bear.

To my shock, I immediately heard sirens coming up to the house, way quicker than I'd expected. At that point, I could hear heavy footsteps as something ran across the great room. As I listened, it sounded like it had gone into the other nearby bedroom, which seemed odd. I quickly opened my bedroom door and ran outside to my car. A sheriff's pickup pulled up, lights flashing, and two deputies got out.

I was so scared I could barely talk, but I finally managed to say that someone had broken into the house. The deputies got out their big search lights and started looking all around. I waited in my car, and they were soon back, saying they hadn't found anything, not even tracks.

Well, I was soon again in the same motel, but this time I decided I wasn't going back to the Fly House. I no longer cared about the money, I just wanted out of there.

So much for my beautiful refuge in the Tetons. At least I felt more resigned about Laura, knowing there really was nothing I could do. Being there had helped with that, though I knew I had a long way to go.

I again spent most of the day in Victor, having lunch at a restaurant there, hanging out at the park, and eventually finding a small cabin for rent. It felt great being away from the Fly House with its big windows and immense feeling of wilderness. I really liked the coziness of the cabin and slept well there my first night.

But the next day I started second-guessing myself, wondering if it really hadn't just been a bear. It was then that I realized I'd left my nice Pendleton jacket at the house. I could easily buy another, but it had been a gift from Laura, and I really wanted it back.

I struggled with the thought of going to get it. I didn't want to go there alone, but since it was broad daylight and I had my bear spray, I decided to go back. I could grab the jacket and get right back out.

Once there, I unlocked the front door and went in, again noting the beautiful views from the great room, and for a moment I wondered if I wasn't just crazy. Why would I leave this beautiful house? Maybe I'd gone over the deep end when Laura left me.

So here I was back at the Fly House, and the windows were again covered with flies. I grabbed my jacket, then quickly walked around the house, making sure I hadn't left anything else, all the while wondering if maybe I should come back.

I finally wandered into the bedroom with the twin beds, which was the only room I really hadn't been in. I have no idea why I went in there, as there was no way I'd left anything, but I guess I just wanted to be sure everything was in order before I left for good.

For some unknown reason, I opened the closet door and found it was a big walk-in closet, but at its back was a deep hole that opened into what looked like a subfloor. I was surprised, for it seemed so out of place in this big beautiful historic house, a dirt hole in one of the closets.

I stood there for the longest time trying to figure it out, and it was then that I noticed flies were starting to come out—lots of flies. It was like they were now coming towards the light when I opened the closet door. I also noticed a strange musty odor that seemed almost overpowering.

As I stood there, I started feeling that same odd lightheaded disoriented feeling, and it made me feel almost dizzy, like I was going to pass out. I started walking backwards and was pulling the door closed when I noticed a big clump of dark hair hanging off one of the door hinges, as if something hairy had pushed its way through. I suddenly felt like I had mere moments to get out of there or I would die.

I turned and ran. I ran through the great room down through the foyer and out the front door, quickly pulling it closed so that whatever was there would have to stop to open it. I jumped in my car and peeled out.

As I drove away, glad to be going to my little cabin in Victor, I knew then that something was indeed there—it wasn't just my imagination or from emotional distress. There was something strange in the Fly House, something malevolent, and it was coming into the house from some kind of tunnel that came out at the root cellar. And whatever it was, it was so disgusting that it attracted flies.

I decided I would never go back, not even to the area, even though it was close to some nice hiking trails in the Teton Valley.

I loved my little cabin in Victor, and after a month, my friend Gary came to visit. He wanted to drive up to Grand Targhee, but I wouldn't go with him, because we'd have to drive by the Fly House. I know he thought I was being dramatic, but there was no way I wanted to go anywhere near there.

The divorce was soon final, and I gave Laura everything she wanted—the house and most of our investments. I just didn't care, and I hoped it would make up for my not being there for her. I wrote her a long letter and sent it to her brother, but I don't know if she ever read it, as I never heard from her again. Gary told me later she was dating a friend of his.

The human mind is the darndest thing, because after all that, whenever I'd think of her, I'd think of being in the Fly House, and I developed an association, and it wasn't a pleasant one. This actually helped me get over her, and after a few months in Victor, a nice place in Driggs came up for rent, and I decided to move there.

I was living on what was left of my savings, and I finally decided I needed to get back to work, so I applied for a job at Grand Targhee on the ski patrol. I'd been up there several times, finally overcoming my fear of driving by the Fly House. I enjoyed the job, though I have to admit that being on a slope with no one around kind of bothered me, but the place was so busy it was unusual to be skiing alone.

I hadn't told anyone I was a doctor, but eventually word got out at how good I was at treating injured people, as most ski injuries are torn ligaments and things I'd dealt with as a surgeon. But I had no desire to get back into the high-stress medical profession, and I was happy living on almost nothing. I even started making a few friends and went on a few dates, though nothing serious.

They say you eventually come back to what you love, and after a couple of years of basically being a ski bum, I saw an on-call position at the hospital in Jackson for an orthopedist. I applied and got it, and it's worked out really well, as I still have lots of time for skiing, though I'm no longer on the ski patrol. But I now make enough money to be able to start saving again, yet I don't have the high stress that goes with being a full-time doctor.

One day, on my way to the ski area, I noticed a backhoe up at the Fly House, and it looked like it was digging up the root cellar. Had the owner discovered what was going on? Not long after, a for-sale sign appeared by the long drive. I wondered why the owner was selling, though I suspected it had something to do with the root cellar. I toyed with the idea of buying it—maybe the creature was gone.

The idea came and went in the short time it took to drive on by, and I knew I would never set foot there again, no matter how beautiful the views. The bad associations there had helped me get over Laura, and that was the only good to come of it. There was no way I could ever go back again.

It sold, and now when I drive by, sometimes I see kids out playing in the yard with their dog. It makes me happy, for I know the creature is gone, probably back into the Jedidiah Smith Wilderness where it belongs, and now the house can be the happy place it should be.

And sometimes when I drive by, I wonder what the current owners would think if they knew their house had once been called the Fly House. I know I'll never be the one to tell them, that's for sure, for I have no intention of ever setting foot on that property again.

6

THE SAWTOOTH SASQUATCH

Andy's a friend of a friend, and when he mentioned his trip into the Sawtooth Range in Idaho to my friend, I soon got wind of it and asked if he'd let me include his story here.

He very graciously said yes, and though there's not much Bigfoot action (or Sasquatch, as he calls them), I found it a compellingly sad story that reveals a side of them we seldom hear about. —Rusty

If I lived a dozen lifetimes, I doubt if I would ever experience anything to top this story, Rusty. It's just one of those things you can't imagine happening to anyone, especially yourself. If I read it in a book, I would laugh and say the guy was nuts. I don't know, maybe you'll feel that way after you hear it. I hope not.

I live in Park City, Utah and work for the parks and recreation department there. It's a very active job, and because of this, I'm in really good shape. You'd think I would prefer to lay around on my days off, but I enjoy hiking and backpacking, which I try to do every weekend in the summer. Since my job's seasonal, I spend the winters working for the ski area doing handyman stuff and whatever needs to be done, then ski on the weekends. All this keeps me in great shape.

Studying maps is kind of my hobby, mostly because I can fantasize about all the cool places I have yet to see and may hopefully visit some day. If I ever get to retire and I'm still physically able, I would happily spend my time backpacking all the places I have marked on maps, with one exception—the Sawtooth Range.

I usually end up in the Wasatch Mountains on weekends, since they're literally my back yard, and I can say I know a lot of that country like the back of my hand. It's beautiful and rugged and has a lot going for it, but when I get more than a weekend off, I always like to see new territory. Unfortunately, I never have enough time to go very far, so I have to plan my trips for the maximum bang for the buck.

The summer this happened, which wasn't long ago, I'd been studying the Sawtooth Range up in Idaho, wondering if I could manage to take a nice backpacking trip up there without using all my vacation time. At a little under 400 miles, the Sawtooths aren't too far from Park City, and if I left on a Friday afternoon after work, I could take the weekend, then add a couple of days off and have a full four-day backpack trip.

Well, I studied the map and did some online research, and I figured out a nice 53-mile loop I could do, which meant I wouldn't need to worry about a car shuttle or trying to hitch a ride back to my car. I'm a strong hiker, and 53 miles would only average a little over 13 miles a day, and maybe I could even get a few miles in on Friday evening, if I could get off work a little early.

A 10-mile hike is really nothing for me, as I've averaged 20 miles or more a day on trips into the Wasatch and Uintas, with lots of vertical. If you keep moving, it isn't that hard to cover 20 miles.

I don't have to accommodate anyone else's schedule because I always hike solo. It's not always by choice—nobody will hike with me because I usually want to go farther than they do. I start early and pretty much hike steady all day, only taking short breaks, and I hike from sunup to sundown, plus I'm not much of one for lounging around camp.

I travel light, like a thru-hiker, which makes a huge difference in how far you can go. I carry a tarp and sleeping bag, my food and water filter, and that's about it, except a nice waterproof jacket.

Another reason I chose the Sawtooths was because they don't have grizzlies. Hiking alone in grizzly country is simply too nerve-wracking for me. In fact, I haven't heard of many hikers there who have even seen black bears, yet alone grizzlies.

Well, I managed to get a couple of days off, and I checked the weather for the Sawtooths, and it called for about two hours of rain starting at midnight the second night I'd be there, with a low reaching 40. A little chilly, but no big deal, as I have a warm bag.

In retrospect, let me say that right then and there I made a huge rookie mistake that almost cost me my life. I don't know what I was thinking, or maybe I wasn't thinking. That report was for the valley, and I was going to be in the mountains. I would normally never make such an assumption, translating valley weather into what was going to happen higher up.

At the last minute, I decided to pack my warm down sweater and wool hat along with my waterproof jacket. I don't know why, but some instinct said to take them.

Anyway, I took off that afternoon straight from work, and it was a drive, but eventually I reached the small town of Stanley, Idaho, though it was well after dark. I drove to the Tin Cup trailhead, where I tried to sleep in my car, which wasn't part of the plan. I had hoped to make a quick camp a ways up the trail, but I had seriously underestimated how long the drive would take, and sleeping in my little Honda didn't work too well.

There was one other car at the trailhead, presumably fellow backpackers who'd come in early enough to get a start. I thought about doing some night hiking, but since I'd worked all day and didn't know the trail, I decided that would be a bad idea.

The next day I found that I'd been wise to wait until daylight, as the trail was extremely rocky with lots of deadfall. It would've been really difficult in the dark.

OK, since I couldn't sleep all cramped up in my car, I thought about my backpacking route. I would start and end there at the Tin Cup trailhead next to Pettit Lake, making a big loop.

I would first hike to Alice Lake, then climb a pass taking me to Toxaway Lake, then over another pass to Edna Lake. After that, I'd go by Hidden Lake and over yet a third pass to Cramer Lake.

Total mileage for that stretch would be over 21 miles with almost 5,000 feet of elevation gain. I actually figured I could do it in one day, but I decided to take it easy and see how it went.

After that stretch, I'd hike from Cramer Lake to Redfish Lake. I knew from reading trip reports that the route out of Redfish was long with a lot of climbing, then you dropped into the Hell Roaring Lake area, then on to Imogene Lake. That distance scaled out to 22 miles with a 4700 feet of elevation gain.

The last stretch was over a pass between Imogene and Edith Lake and was only 10 miles back to the trailhead and my car. I'd pass Farley Lake and take a trail from Yellow Belly Lakes back to the Tin Cup trailhead at Pettit Lake.

My grand tour would cover 53 miles with lots of ups and downs, but I was in excellent shape and had no worries. In retrospect, it sounds really hard, but like I said, I enjoy hiking, and I just go steady and conquer all.

Anyway, as I lay there all scrunched up, I had to laugh. It was like a tour of Sawtooth lakes! Of course, about everywhere you go in the Sawtooth there are lots of lakes, primarily because the range is heavily glaciated with lots of cirques and tarns. In fact, the range has several hundred lakes, many unnamed and frozen over until late summer. Glaciation is what gave the range the look of a sawtooth, with lots of arêtes and sharp ridges.

Even though there in my car I told myself no worries, I would've had plenty of worries if I'd been able to look into the future. Actually, if I could see the future, I would've turned around and gone home that same night.

I tossed and turned all night—or I should say I tried to toss and turn, but was so confined I could barely move. More than once, I felt like I should just give up. Maybe I would be better off just taking a nice quiet four-day vacation, drive around the nearby areas of Ketchum and Sun Valley, and go for some nice mellow hikes.

Something was tugging at my mind, something that might have been a bit of foresight—or maybe it was my instincts telling me a bad storm was coming in. I really wish now I'd listened.

I was up early, and it looked like it was going to be a gorgeous sunny day. I almost left my hat and down sweater in the car, it looked so nice, but I decided at the last minute to take them, knowing the weatherman was usually right.

I was soon making my way up the rocky trail, going over and around deadfall, wondering why the forest service didn't do a better job of maintenance. The scenery was pretty, but not as spectacular as I knew it would get once I was higher and could see out more.

It was around 10 a.m. when I came upon a pair of backpackers on their way out, two guys who looked to be in their 30s. They stopped and visited for a minute, then asked if I was aware that bad weather was coming in. One of the guy's wives had managed to get them on their phone and tell them the forecast, and they were heading out early. The storm would hit that night.

I nodded sagely, saying I knew, thinking to myself that they were easily dissuaded, as it didn't sound like much of a storm. They asked if I was sure I wanted to continue and remarked that it didn't look like I was all that well-prepared for bad weather, traveling so light.

This last comment irritated me, for to me it implied I was a rookie, but I didn't say anything. Of course, as these things go, I later had to admit they were right.

I was soon at Alice Lake, where I could now see a panorama of the Sawtooths, and they reminded me a little of Yosemite with its huge gray granite batholiths. The Sawtooth Range has over 50 peaks higher than 11,000 feet, and many of them are ragged with lots of spires.

Now climbing the pass to Toxaway Lake, I had a magnificent view down onto Twin Lakes, which I stopped to enjoy. The Sawtooths were turning out to be more scenic than I'd imagined, and I wished

I'd brought my little pocket camera, something I'd left behind to make my pack lighter.

But as I sat there on a big white rock, I had a strange sensation come over me—I felt like I should turn around and go back. I'd never felt like that. Usually I'm so buzzed on endorphins from the hike that I feel nothing but excitement.

I could now see a low line of dark clouds to the west in the far distance, like a long smudge on a landscape painting, and I knew it was the storm coming in. It looked much worse than a few hours of rain, it was so black. And it was early! The storm wasn't supposed to hit until about midnight, but it looked like it was much closer. Of course, I knew I was up high enough that I could see a long ways, so that was a factor.

I was eventually at Toxaway Lake, then on the pass to Edna Lake. I stopped to eat a bite and regain some energy, and I again noted the black clouds, looking more and more ominous. Should I turn around?

I can be a little compulsive when I hike, probably another reason nobody will hike with me. I decided I'd try to get to Cramer Lake before dark, which would be over one-third of the total distance at 21 miles.

The elevation gain was starting to get to me, but I just kicked into second gear and went on. I don't know—maybe I was thinking if I did the hike in super fast time I would outrun the storm, which made no sense at all, as it was scheduled to hit that night. What it would do is ensure I was as deep in the Sawtooth Wilderness as I could get when the storm hit.

By evening, I was in a basin above Cramer Lake, winding my way through endless scree and rubble from rock glaciers and erosion. It was tremendously slow going, but my spirits were lifted when I saw a mountain goat above me on the rocky hillside.

I'd soon crossed the third pass and was at Cramer Lake, where I would spend the night. It was late evening, and the lake seemed lonely. It's only about a quarter-mile in length and width, not a really big lake, and it felt really high and remote, though its altitude at over 8,000 feet was only a thousand feet higher than Park City.

I found a nice section of trees near the lake where I could tie my tarp for shelter, then set about gathering wood for a fire. I usually have a fire only when cooking, as I don't like to carry a stove, and it doesn't take much wood to boil water, which I'll filter from whatever source is nearby.

For some reason, I gathered extra wood and stacked it under my tarp. I guess I knew it would soon be storming and figured I might need some warmth. In fact, I gathered quite a lot, barely leaving room to lay out my sleeping bag and pad.

The sky was clear, but I was down in somewhat of a bowl and couldn't see to the horizon, like I'd been able to up on the pass. I knew the storm would soon be there, but I would enjoy the night sky until it clouded up, then just go to bed. My tarp would keep me dry unless water started running in under me, but since I'd selected a bit of a rise for my camp, that was unlikely.

While eating my freeze-dried lasagna, I noted there was no wind, which was a good sign. A big storm would have a big wind before it, so I trusted that the forecast for just a small amount of rain would be accurate.

After dinner, I decided to walk down to the lake. I slipped from the forest and went to the lake's edge, where I sat down, watching the last ray's of sunlight reflect off the water.

Everything seemed so peaceful, and I knew I was the only person around for who knows how many miles. I noted how calm it seemed to be—was it the calm before the storm?

As I sat there, I started feeling like something was off. It was calm, but almost eerily calm. There were no wilderness sounds at all—no birds, no owls, not even one cricket chirping. It made me hesitate—was it from the oncoming storm? Did the animals sense the change in barometric pressure?

Just then, I noticed someone on the other shore of the lake! They seemed unaware of my presence, and for some reason I felt the need to move back behind a rock.

As I watched, a second person stepped out of the shadows, and they seemed to be conversing, arms gesticulating, though I could hear no sound—of course, they were a good quarter-mile away. Soon, one picked up a rock and threw it into the lake. It looked like a large rock, though I couldn't hear the splash. I was surprised at how strong they'd have to be to pick it up.

Now the other picked up a rock and threw it in, and they were soon tossing rocks around like baseballs. I wanted to smile, as it seemed like they were having fun, but there was something about it that seemed off—I couldn't put my finger on why I should feel that way. I figured they hadn't seen me, or maybe they would've come over to talk. It was just as well, as I was tired.

As it got darker, they pulled back into the shadows and disappeared, and I returned to my tarp shelter. I slipped on my warm down sweater and wool hat, then climbed into my bag, where I lay very still, listening, but there were no sounds of anything, no talking, no breeze, nothing. It still felt unnatural and eerie.

I soon relaxed, thinking that around midnight I'd probably wake to a couple of hours of rain. The temperature would drop to 40, then the next day should be nice, as it would've all blown through by morning.

I had to hunker down to stay warm, and it dawned on me that it was already 40 degrees, and maybe even colder. Thinking about it, it felt about like it had on my last overnighter in the Uintas, and that had been 36 degrees, according to the little thermometer clipped to my pack.

I suddenly sat up, realizing my mistake. The weather forecast had to have been for the valley, not the mountains. Rain and 40 degrees on the valley floor would look a lot different at 8,000 feet. And a short storm could move quickly through the valley while hammering the mountains for a long time. I'd seen it many times in the Wasatch—a storm sweeping through the valley then hanging over the mountains for a day or two.

I immediately knew I'd made a mistake, one that could potentially cost me my life. I wasn't prepared for snow, especially deep snow. It occurred to me that I should try to hike out now, even though it was dark. I had a good headlamp.

But a lot of the route wasn't technically on a trail, it was just scrambling through rocks and scree, and one needed to be able to see where they were going. It would all look the same by headlamp, and it would be easy to get lost or to even go in circles. Parts of the trail were well-enough defined, but the parts that weren't could be suicidal.

Besides, I was really tired. There had been no reason to push like I had, and now I was paying the price. I couldn't hike out if I had to.

All I could do was sleep and wait it out. I was hopefully making it out to be much worse than it would be. There was no wind, and I could still see the stars. And I had enough wood to last quite awhile, if I was frugal. I finally slipped into a fitful sleep.

I dreamed that I was on the shore of a large lake in the Sawtooths, watching as it started to snow. I was surprised, for the snow had come in really hard and fast, more like a cloud of fast-moving dust than snow.

As the cloud came nearer, I realized it was indeed dust and would soon overtake me, making it impossible to breathe. I started running, but I knew there was no way I could outrun it, and I soon dropped to the ground, holding my arms over my head for protection.

I quickly woke, struggling to breathe, then realized I was all caught up in my down sweater, having somehow pulled the waist up onto my head. I pulled it back down and could breathe again, but I had no idea where I was. All I knew was that it was pitch dark, and I could hear the clatter of rocks in the distance.

I finally remembered that I was camped by Cramer Lake. Strange that the two guys would be throwing rocks into the water in the middle of the night, I thought, then realized the sound was way too loud. I had to be hearing actual rockfall coming from the nearby cliffs.

I paused and thought back, trying to recall where I'd placed my camp—was I close enough to the cliffs to be in danger? What was going on?

Now the sound of rockfall increased, and I realized the ground was shaking. It was an earthquake!

The shaking lasted maybe 20 seconds, and I knew as soon as it stopped that it hadn't been a serious quake, for big earthquakes typically last a long time, even several minutes.

I slipped from my bag, listening to try to determine where the rockfall was, but I knew it was hopeless in terms of trying to outrun it. It was dark, and rockslides can go over 100 miles per hour. All I could do was wait it out. It gradually petered out and stopped, though I could still hear an occasional rock falling.

I got out of my bag and leaned on the pile of wood I'd stacked, feeling lucky I hadn't been in the avalanche's path, wondering if there was more shaking to come.

I thought about what I knew about earthquakes. Living in the Wasatch Range, I'd done a fair amount of research, as the Wasatch Fault has a high probability for quakes. I'd also read about the Sawtooths, for they also have high earthquake potential. Both regions are part of the Basin and Range Province, which is slowly being stretched and pulled apart by tectonic forces.

I knew I was practically on top of the Sawtooth Fault, which was 40 miles long and runs under Redfish Lake, which was on my hiking itinerary. It hadn't been all that long ago that a 6.5 quake had hit the area, resulting in a lot of avalanches and reshaping of the Sawtooths, including toppling rock-climbing destinations like the Baron Spire and the Finger of Fate, damaging the lava tubes at nearby Craters of the Moon, and piling rock debris over some of the trails.

In addition, a trail near Redfish Lake had to be rerouted because of a boulder the size of a two-story house, and a number of big walls had sheared off, such as the east face of Grand Mogul. The Alice-Toxaway section of trail, which I'd just come over, had been particularly hard hit.

Of course! I now realized that the difficulty I'd had with all the scree and rockfall was probably from the earthquake or from one of the hundreds of its aftershocks, one of which I'd probably just experienced.

I'd been so busy worrying about the weather that I'd failed to remember what I'd read about the trails. I now recalled how one ranger had said to look for trees around your campsite loosened by the quakes and could fall, and to make sure you're not camped under a steep slope that could collapse. I hadn't even bothered to look for unstable trees or steep slopes, I'd just made camp.

Suddenly, a loud *whump* roused me from my thoughts, making me jump. It sounded like a rock had come down right by my camp, but I soon realized it was wet snow sliding from my tarp. It hadn't rained at all, which would've probably woken me, but instead had quietly snowed.

I looked out to see it was snowing hard, maybe a good two inches an hour, a full-on driving snowstorm, with a good eight inches or so on the ground. At this rate, I'd need snowshoes to get out!

I spent the rest of the night smacking the underside of the tarp to break up the heavy snow, which would then slide down the sides and pile up in front of me and the wood. At least it provided a nice wind break, once it got deep enough.

And fortunately, it wasn't all that cold, though I knew the cold would come when the storm passed and the skies cleared. Hopefully, that would be the following morning, and I could hike out. I'd already decided to go back the way I'd come.

I tried to ignore the dangers of the situation and focus on knocking the snow off the tarp, huddled under it, listening to the storm, wondering if there would be more rockfall.

My thoughts went to the two fellows down by the lake, and I wondered how they were faring. Had they been in the path of the rockslide? Maybe when it got light enough to see I should go check on them, though I wasn't really sure where their camp was.

Well, I can say that there in my bag, reaching up with a stick every so often to push the snow off, really put the meaning into the phrase, "It was the longest night." I thought it would never end—or stop snowing.

With dawn, I could start to make out the shapes of the nearby trees and that the snow had finally stopped. It had snowed a good 18 inches.

I quickly built a tiny fire and made some hot tea and oatmeal, then packed everything up and made ready to leave. I knew it would be a long haul to get back to my car, maybe even impossible in one day, as I'd had to really push to get there, and it would be difficult to hike back out the 20-plus miles in the snow. At least it would be downhill.

I will say that once the sun rose up over the mountains, it was one of the most beautiful sights I've ever seen. The heavy wet snow had become white powder covering everything—and behind it was the most amazing purple sunrise imaginable, giving everything a lavender tint. I was awestruck, trying to record it in my memory, once again wishing I'd brought my camera.

Yet I'll always associate that beauty with one of the weirdest things I've ever experienced.

As I stood, taking in the incredible sight, I heard a sound coming from down by the lake, a sound that I can only describe as a keening, a heart-rending wailing that came from deep grief. I'd heard a similar sound only once before when I'd been with a friend mourning her young child's death, and I hope to never hear it again.

I kicked my way through the deep snow until I could see down to the lake. There stood one of the figures I'd seen the night before, and I knew it was the source of the sound. As I watched, it carefully picked up and stacked nearby rocks while moaning and wailing. I was again amazed at the size of the rocks and at how easily the person picked them up.

I felt very sad, wondering if the other one had been killed in the rockslide. Looking back up to the source of the rockslide, I could see it had narrowly missed my camp, and I felt incredibly lucky. And now I watched as the figure moved one last rock, then turned and began walking through the snow up to the pass over to Hidden Lake.

I was amazed at how easily they seemed to walk through the rocks and deep snow, and I knew I should follow their path, as it would make things much easier for me. And though earlier I'd been concerned about them, I now had no desire to meet them or have them know I was there.

I wanted to give them plenty of time to get ahead of me, so I waited, then decided to walk down to the lakeshore and see where the avalanche had hit. Once there, I could see where the person had been stacking rocks.

I felt sick, wondering if the body of their friend was under the rocks. I thought back to how I'd watched them play the evening before and felt an immense sense of loss, even though I'd never met them. Life seemed so transitory, and I knew mine could easily end if I couldn't hike out, for I knew it was going to get bitter cold that night and I wasn't prepared.

I turned to go, but not before a patch of brown caught my eye. There, under the rocks but not quite buried was part of a foot. It was obviously a foot, but the part sticking out was covered with thick brown hair.

I almost choked. No wonder they were picking up the rocks so easily! They weren't human! I now felt an urgency to get out of there and back to my car, and I regretted having come in so far the first day. I could never get out in this deep snow as quickly as I'd come in, no matter how good my endurance.

Now I started following the path left by the other creature. The tracks were so large that they'd created a nice trail, and no wonder, if this one had feet like the other. I struggled to come up with what I was dealing with—somehow I knew they had to be Sasquatch, and yet my mind just couldn't accept it.

And one was just ahead of me! What if I managed to catch up to it? Would it harm me? And yet I had no choice but to try to make the best time I possibly could.

I followed those tracks all the way to Hidden Lake, on to Toxaway Lake, then to Edna Lake, where I stopped to eat a bite and recover. I was making much better time than I thought I would, thanks to the tracks and it being downhill. But it wasn't long before the tracks veered off the route, and I knew the Sasquatch had gone its own way.

I felt a sense of relief, knowing I wouldn't run into it, yet I knew the going would now become much more difficult.

About two or three miles from the trailhead, I sat down on a log, exhausted and depressed, wondering if I could survive the night, for I didn't think I was going to make it out. Darkness was falling, and I knew I'd made the potentially fatal mistake of underestimating the weather, and I would now pay the price. I was too tired to even think of making another camp and collecting enough wood to get me through the night, plus it was all wet from the snow.

I could see my breath in the cold air and felt it beginning to seep through my clothes. I wanted to cry, wondering if they'd find my body frozen solid like the log I was sitting on, and I felt a great loss at leaving my life so young. Would I be like the Sasquatch buried under the rocks in the rockslide—one day happy and carefree, and the next day gone?

It was then that I again heard the keening and heart-breaking wailing far in the distance, and I knew I had to press on. I could do this—I could conjure up the energy I needed to go a few more miles.

I finally arrived at the Tin Cup trailhead long after dark, glad for my headlamp and the chocolate I'd brought for instant energy. I was exhausted, but at least by then the snow wasn't as deep and the trail was easier to follow. The temperature was already dropping when I got to my car, and I knew it would be a bitter cold night.

I was too tired to drive home, so I got a room in Ketchum. The warmth and safety of the room almost felt surreal, and that night I dreamed of rockfall and Sasquatch and the Baron Spire collapsing in a cloud of dust.

I'd survived my rookie expedition into the Sawtooths, an adventure I would never forget, complete with earthquake, snow, and Sasquatch. Any one of the three is enough for an adventure, but all three at once was too much, and I've never gone back.

And to think I was afraid of meeting a lowly grizzly bear.

7
STAY JUST A LITTLE BIT LONGER

I met Marie at the Bighorn County Rodeo Queen Contest in Basin, Wyoming, where she was one of the judges.

What was I doing there? Well, my wife Sarah and I were taking a new way home to Colorado from Bozeman, Montana, where I sometimes help a friend do flyfishing workshops, and Sarah noticed the contest was going on at the fairgrounds, so we had to stop.

Sarah's niece is a barrel racer, which is one of the criteria they use for selecting rodeo queens. I admit I was kind of irritated, just wanting to get home, but it actually ended up being a lot of fun. These young women are real athletes, along with their horses.

After the contest was over, we mingled a bit with the crowd, Sarah being her gregarious self, and we got to meet Marie. Come to find out, her late husband Bill was an avid flyfisherman. She invited us to come stay at her beautiful ranch, which was a real treat, being in sight of the big mountains in Yellowstone.

When I asked why she had a hot-wire fence around her house, Marie told this story. We all sat on her front porch watching the sunset, and after she was finished, none of us really wanted to go inside, though we were kind of spooked, to be honest. But in spite of that, we had hopes of seeing her unusual friends, though luck wasn't with us. We did sleep like babies that

night in her spare room, in spite of what she told us hung out nearby.
—*Rusty*

My name's Marie, and I live near the small town of Clark, Wyoming, which is along the eastern edge of the Absaroka Mountains, which many of you will recognize as the range that goes through Yellowstone National Park. To the west is the Bighorns, which aren't as extensive or tall as the Absarokas, but are incredible in their own right, with mountains like aptly named Cloud Peak.

There's quite a bit of distance between the two ranges, a large flat valley with lots of sagebrush and ranches and small towns. If you've ever been to Cody, Wyoming, the eastern entrance to Yellowstone, you've been near Clark, which is just north of there.

So, picture a small older farm house on 300 acres of grass hay near the Clark Fork tributary of the Yellowstone River with mountains in both directions, and you've got my house. It's a modest place, just two small bedrooms and one bath, with a nice deck that goes all the way around it so I can enjoy the views in all directions.

That deck was built by my son-in-law, Jeff, who lives with my daughter Carla and grandkids in the town of Clark itself. I'm actually a few miles out of town. Jeff works all over the area as a large-animal veterinarian, doctoring horses and cattle and such. Carla pretty much stays home with the kids, who are still pretty young, though she raises chickens and sells their eggs.

This means she probably has more time on her hands than she needs, and I think she spends it thinking of ways to boss me around —well, used to anyway. I eventually had to shut that down, which she didn't like one bit, but it's all worked out, as you'll see.

OK, I shouldn't be so blunt, as I love her dearly, but at one point, she played a part in some ongoing mental problems I had, problems that seem to be more common than people want to believe. I'm talking about depression, which some think is just feeling bad, but it's way more than that, as you basically disengage from living your life.

I never had any problems with depression before my husband Bill died. He and I were very happy together, married 42 years, then he had to go and have a heart attack. Gone, just like that.

Bill and I were the co-owners of the Two Heart Ranch, which raised the best Black Angus cattle you could buy. We eventually got to where we raised only breeding stock, having cut back significantly from grazing stock. Now I don't have any stock at all and lease the ranch out for hay.

Raising stock is hard work, and it was getting to where we'd have to watch for grizzlies, who were starting to poach our calves, which got real discouraging, even though the Wyoming wildlife department would pay for them.

The Absaroka range is home to a good number of grizzly bears, which are originally plains animals but were driven to the high country by early settlers and stockmen like us. The original grizzly habitat stretched clear into the midwest, and maybe even farther east, as far as I know.

Recently, grizzlies started coming more and more down into the lowlands, like the country around Clark. In fact, we had a fellow mauled and nearly killed not too long ago, and he was just walking in the sagebrush flats, not even thinking about bears.

OK, I know you're wondering what all this—grizzly bears, depression—has to do with Bigfoot, but I'm getting there. I'm 72 years old, so my brain has lots of information in it, and I sometimes get derailed and have to get back on track. Actually, I'm not derailed, I'm just taking the long way around.

Bill and I got married when I was 20, so most of my life was spent with him by my side. I was 63 when he passed, and I was still in pretty good shape, still working alongside him on the ranch. But with him gone, there was no way I could run it alone, even with our hired guy, Lee. So, the first thing my daughter decided after Bill passed, with no input from me at all, was that I would sell the Two Heart.

That ranch was my heart and soul, as well as Bill's, which is why we called it the Two Heart. Bill and I had built it up from the 200 acres his folks had homesteaded into a holding of over 3,000 acres, plus some of the best grazing rights in the state of Wyoming. To lose Bill and the ranch both was just too much.

I told Carla there was no way I was selling it. She said she had my best interests in mind, but I wondered if she just wanted to see me cash out, as it was worth a fortune. This was when rich people started coming into Wyoming and buying up these big ranches all over the place for investments and tax write-offs.

I'll never forget it—sitting on the deck one evening with Carla and the kids and her showing me pictures on her computer of all these glorious vacation places I would be able to afford to visit after I'd sold out and was rich. And she and the kids would come along, too, of course.

I had no interest in going to Cancun or Disneyland or whatever. None at all. I loved the ranch, I loved the herd of deer that would come right up to the house in the evenings, and I loved my two horses, which were the offspring of the mighty Painted Heart, the Paint stallion who had sired many a champion right there on the ranch when I had him standing at stud. The ranch was my life.

Carla gave up trying to talk me into selling, though every once in awhile she'd get in a barb or two about how I was working too hard and how she worried I would hurt myself or some such nonsense. There were times she left me wanting to cry, saying I was stubborn and was going to end up in a nursing home.

Well, I *am* stubborn, but I always thought it was in a good way, the kind of stubborn where I could do whatever needed doing. I held on for several years, ranching, though I could see my time was coming.

I think one of the hardest days of my life was when I tried to get on my old gelding, Rebel, and I was so arthritic I could no longer get my leg across his back. I tried several times, but it was a no go.

I finally led him over to the fence and got on that way, but I knew our time as riding buddies was coming to an end. Riding had always been my therapy when I got down, and I didn't know what I would do.

It didn't help when a few months later I found him out in the pasture, unable to get up, and I had to have Carla's husband come and put him down. It was only a few weeks later that Sammy, my other gelding, died, maybe of a broken heart, as he and Rebel were lifelong buddies, just like me and Bill.

Oh geez, I know this is getting depressing, and I apologize! But it has a good ending, let me assure you, so stick around.

Things began to deteriorate further, and I knew some of it was from my attitude, as it was going to heck fast. And Carla wasn't helping things. I got to where I avoided her, though I wanted to see the kids, as they always cheered me up. But she'd always talk about what was I going to do when this or that happened and how I should sell the ranch while the economy was good and I could get top dollar for it.

The icing on the cake was when I had a knock on my door and a real-estate gal from Cody introduced herself, saying my daughter had asked her to come talk to me. I was polite, though I wasn't too happy, and when she left, she said she'd get back to me with a market analysis.

I should've been furious with Carla, but I was beginning to give up. I could feel my health starting to deteriorate—lots of arthritic pain and a low-level headache that wouldn't go away. I also found myself reminiscing about the good old days, going through old pictures and such, which was unlike me. My life was slowing down.

That market analysis was pretty mind-blowing. The Two Heart was worth millions. I couldn't even process how much money that was. The real-estate woman said I could sell it as a working ranch and the hired guy would probably be able to keep his job, as she knew I felt a loyalty to him. The fact that it had priority water rights added to the value, as well as its many acres of premium hay fields.

Let me add at this point that most of the West was in a drought at that time and still is. Those water rights were very valuable, as they guaranteed the ranch would always have water, as long as there was water to be had. Some nearby ranchers who had junior rights were already having problems having sufficient irrigation water and were having to let their fields go fallow and cut back on how much stock they raised.

Finding out what the Two Heart was worth really threw me for a loop. Maybe I should sell out. But what would I do with all that money? I could buy me a little place in Clark or even Cody and bank the rest, leave it to Carla when I died.

Well, now I had the real-estate woman on my case, along with Carla, both bugging me to sell. I'm a pretty patient person, but it was starting to get to me. I can look back now and see it clearly, but at the time I didn't make the connection between the stress and my health. Their constant barrage, plus Carla always telling me I was getting too old to run the ranch, was taking its toll.

In actuality, I did feel like I was getting too old, and I ended up giving my hired guy Lee more and more responsibilities, as I felt worse and worse. I was getting more stoved up, and now my right shoulder was starting to ache constantly, as well as my knees. And some days I'd be too fatigued to even want to get out of bed.

Well, things were slowly deteriorating, with no hope in sight, and thinking about selling the ranch just made me worse. I know a lot of people would've felt better, looking forward to all that money and being able to retire, but like I said, the ranch was my life. I knew once the ranch was gone, I would be a goner, too.

But things were changing, though I didn't realize it. One late summer evening, my working dog Annie and I were sitting out on the porch, watching the last rays of light hit the mountaintops, just enjoying the view, when I felt a sudden chill.

At exactly the same moment, Annie let out a low growl, then got up and started for the open door. But instead of going in, she stood and waited, watching me, as if wanting me to follow. I know Annie well, as I've had her since a pup, and her body language speaks volumes.

I stood and walked to the door, then turned to look. There was something way out in the field, and it looked like a bear. I went inside and got my bear spray, then closed all the windows and watched.

Like I said, young grizzlies were coming into that part of Wyoming more and more from the Greater Yellowstone Ecosystem, looking for their own territory, pushed out by the older bears. The same problem was going on up in eastern Montana along the Highline, and ranchers there were also losing more and more stock.

I called Lee, my ranch hand, and told him there was a bear in the front pasture, and he said to keep an eye on it until he could get there. He'd try to haze it away with some kind of firecrackers the wildlife people gave him—bear bangers, they're called.

Since I no longer had livestock in that pasture—it was now a hay field—I told him not to bother, that I'd call again if it came close, but so far it wasn't doing any harm. He seemed put out, wondering why I'd called him, and I told him I just thought it was a good idea for someone to know.

Me and Annie watched that bear until it was close enough I could tell it was a grizzly. Darn! Black bears will run, but grizzlies are not easily frightened. I didn't want it around, more for its own sake, as I knew it would eventually lead to trouble of some kind or another. I decided I should've let Lee come and haze it away.

I was getting ready to call Lee back when I saw something else way out in the pasture, something black, much darker than the bear. Was it a black bear? How odd to see both kinds at once, since it was unusual to see a bear of either type. I strained to see what it was, all the while keeping an eye on the grizzly, which had now ambled closer to the house, seeming to have nary a care in the world.

Now I could tell the black thing was made up of a low part and a higher part, which I know is an odd way to describe something, but it was puzzling. It then dawned on me that it had to be a buffalo! That's what the low part was, its hindquarters.

Things were getting interesting! We never had buffalo come around. It must have wandered over from Yellowstone. I probably should call Lee, for a buffalo could quickly cause damage to the hay. And yes, I know they're supposed to be called bison now, but we old-timers still call them buffalo.

I grabbed my binoculars. I was having a field day, right here at the window of my own house, a grizzly and a buffalo at the same time. Why would anyone want to leave a place like this? It was better than being in Yellowstone, for I had all the comforts of home while watching the megafauna, as the park calls the big animals."

The griz was now close enough to the house, just loping across the field, and Annie was getting nervous, letting out a short sharp bark every so often to warn me, up on a chair by the window. I calmed her down by talking softly, saying, "It's OK, Annie, it's OK."

But about then it dawned on me that it wasn't OK. The griz was now coming straight for the house, and even though I had bear spray, I wasn't so sure about having a bear around. I had my rifle, but there was no way I wanted to shoot it. Would it actually try to come inside? It didn't look like it had any bad intentions or anything, just ambling along.

I was watching it through my binoculars, amazed at how beautiful its thick blonde coat was when I remembered the buffalo. It took me a minute to find it, as it had also moved across the field, and I recall thinking how fast it was. I'd heard they can run up to 30 miles per hour, but I wondered why it wasn't stopping to eat the lush hay. What was the hurry?

I then realized something odd had happened—it had broken in two! The smaller part was now running near the bigger part, and I realized it wasn't a buffalo at all, but a mama and young bear. Great—a bear convention, right in my yard. It was interesting seeing them, but weren't bears solitary? Why was the pair seemingly following the griz, and were they also grizzlies? They seemed to be too black.

Now the first bear wasn't more than 100 feet from my front door, and Annie was now really carrying on, whining and barking, ignoring my trying to soothe her. But suddenly the bear stopped and turned, as if realizing something was behind it. It stood on its hind legs to get a better look, then turned and bolted on all fours over to the side of the field, disappearing behind a small rise. It happened so fast I didn't get a chance to grab my camera, which had been my plan if it got close enough.

Now the other two were running also, but in the opposite direction, back where they'd come from. It's as if they hadn't known the griz was there until it cut across the field to where they saw it. I grabbed my binoculars just in time to see their rear ends disappear across the field.

Annie now seemed to calm down, and I went to the kitchen and got her a biscuit. The excitement was over. As I was feeding her, gazing at the field and half-expecting to see something else, it dawned on me that the two bears had been walking on their hind legs the entire time, which was very unusual.

The view I'd had of them was brief, but I had noted how black they were and how thick the big one's back seemed to be, kind of like a sumo wrestler. Oh, and another odd thing was that their heads seemed to be kind of shaped like someone wearing a hoodie, just a tad elongated.

It was all catching up with me, and I began feeling really unsettled. I decided to call Lee and tell him what I'd seen, and he called just then, as if reading my mind.

"Marie, did that bear leave? I've been worried."

"Lee, I think it's gone. It's OK, but thanks."

Now he paused, and I could tell he was wanting to say something. He always got real quiet before talking about important things.

"Can I come over? I need to talk to you."

I somehow knew he wanted to talk about me selling the ranch. Had Carla been bugging him, too?

"Come on over."

Lee lived in a modular on the other side of the ranch, a couple of miles away. His kids were all grown and he lived alone, his wife having divorced him long ago. It seemed he had a tendency to tie one on every once in a while, though it had never been a problem from my viewpoint, as he worked hard and was reliable and only drank on his days off.

It was getting dark, and I was relieved to see his pickup lights coming up the lane. The thought of having someone around seemed comforting.

He pulled up and ran into the house. I couldn't help but smile, knowing the bear was long gone, but when I saw his face, I knew he was dead serious. He was worried about the bear, but I could also tell this was about more than a bear coming into the field.

He got right to the point.

"Marie, Carla says she's trying to talk you into selling, and I think you should. I'm old enough to retire, and it would suit me just fine. I can go stay with my brother over in Basin."

"I thought you were coming over to talk about the bear," I replied, changing the subject.

"That bear is exactly why I think you should sell the place."

"Sell because of a bear? It didn't even stick around. Don't tell me you're that scared of bears, Lee. It's not like you."

"I'm plenty scared of bears, Marie, like everyone should be. But that bear is just a forerunner. We've all heard the stories about grizzlies moving back down from the mountains. Things are getting too crowded."

"A forerunner? Of what?"

"Marie, what exactly did you see out there? A grizzly?"

"Well, of course, that's why I called you."

Did Lee somehow know about the other things I'd seen? Did he know what they were?

"Things are changing, Marie. Something strange is afoot. It would be prudent to leave."

"Do you want to leave, Lee? You've lived here a good part of your life."

"I used to love it here, just like you do. But it's getting to where I'm afraid more often than not. There's more than bears moving down out of the mountains, something I'd rather not deal with."

Well, this wasn't at all how I thought the conversation would go. I really didn't want to talk about selling the ranch, but we did, and we talked far into the night. Lee ended up sleeping in my guest room. Neither of us wanted to admit it, but we didn't want to be alone.

It felt good to have someone around, I'll admit, much more secure, and it made me miss Bill. I missed him even more when, in the middle of the night, Annie started growling and moved from her regular place at the foot of my bed up next to my pillow, as if she wanted to protect me—or maybe she was scared.

I quietly got up and pulled the curtain back a bit, but it was too dark to see anything. Just then, I heard a tap on my bedroom door. It was Lee, and he whispered, asking me if everything was OK.

Now, Lee and I have known each other since we were kids, though he's a few years younger than me. We're good friends, even though he works for me and I occasionally have to remind him of that, as he can be bull-headed. But we trust each other implicitly, and I could tell he was scared.

"Marie, you know I mentioned things coming down out of the mountains. I didn't want to worry you. but they've been coming over to my house, and now I think they're here."

"You mean the black things I saw? What do you think they are?"

"I don't know, but maybe Bigfoot. Don't laugh, but I've seen a couple of them over by the barn, and that's what they have to be."

"Are they dangerous?"

"I don't know."

"How can something like that even exist? Surely there would be proof by now."

We were whispering this entire time, the lights out, and Annie started growling again. She was staring at the window, as if there was something out there! Lee slowly walked over and slipped the curtain back, just as I'd done, but now we could see a set of big yellow eyes looking in at us.

He quickly pulled the curtain closed.

"Where's your rifle, Marie? Mine's in my truck, and I'm sure not going out there."

"You can't shoot something just for looking in the window."

"Heck if I can't."

I was worried sick, but didn't want to show it. "Let's go out and offer them some tea, be good neighbors."

"Surely you're joking," Lee replied incredulously, then started laughing. It broke the tension, and he came and sat down by me.

"Marie, sell this place. Tomorrow."

"Let's not be hasty. They could be harmless. How do you know it wasn't that grizzly?"

He answered, "Didn't you notice how the eyes shined? There's no moonlight. It's like the eyes have their own light source. It's creepy. Besides, do you want something like that looking through your window at night, harmless or not?"

He had a point.

I asked, "Has anyone else been seeing them?"

"I don't know. It's not something people want to talk about."

Annie finally relaxed, so I figured it was gone. I sighed, motioning Lee to come with me into the kitchen. It was almost dawn, so I started a pot of coffee. We both sat at the table, not saying much, still half asleep.

Finally, as the sun rose, Lee walked around, looking out all the windows, then said, "I think they're gone. I should get on home. Marie, I think you should come over to my place for a few days until these things move on."

"I may do just that," I said, as he hesitantly walked out to his truck, then drove off.

It wasn't ten minutes before he was back.

"Let's just pack up your stuff and go now," he said. "They could come back anytime. I'll help you, just tell me what you need to take. I'll get Annie's dog food."

I really didn't want to go to Lee's. I liked my comfy house, but he sounded so worried, I decided he had a point. I started packing a few things in a suitcase, but just then, my shoulder seized up, and I dropped the bag.

Lee was concerned, saying, "Carla said you're having some health problems, and I have to say you haven't been looking like your old self, dear. Let me carry that."

Oh boy. For my hired hand to call me dear was insubordination in my book. I wasn't anybody's "dear." To me, it was like calling me a sweet little old lady. I might be getting old, but I'd be darned if I'd be sweet. It felt too personal.

"I've changed my mind, Lee," I said. "I'm staying here. I can deal with whatever it is. I've taken care of myself all my life, and I'm not going to stop now. And I'm not selling the Two Heart. You can retire any time you want—I won't hold you to working here if you don't want to, you know that."

Lee knows me, and he knew better than to argue. He shrugged his shoulders and left, saying to call him if I needed anything.

It was a beautiful day, and I was now feeling that our fears of the previous night had just fed on each other and were overhyped. I'd do better alone. Annie could tell me if anything was going on. I'd get my rifle out where it would be handy.

I ran into town and got some groceries, then went home and sat on the front deck. I was feeling much better, my arthritis not nearly as bad. I wondered if it had anything to do with feeling like I was taking control of my life back.

As I sat there, it occurred to me that maybe Lee had been part of a conspiracy by Carla to get me to leave my house. It was too obvious—move in with him, let him take care of everything, making me weaker and more dependent on someone else.

Ha! Foiled them. I was starting to get mad at the thought. I didn't like the thought of him and Carla ganging up on me. I finally decided to call him and clear the air, let him know I was on to them.

I felt a surge of my old self go through me, my old independence and sense of agency. I could do whatever I wanted, within reason. Sure, I was getting older, but so what? I'd die on my own two feet, right here on the Two Heart.

Well, the call didn't go so well. Lee was very sorry and assured me he and Carla weren't up to anything. If I wanted, he'd be glad to move in with me and let me take care of him. Good old Lee, always the wit, but I knew he was being honest.

I sat there, thinking, for what seemed like hours, trying to determine my own fate. Maybe I should sell. Maybe I wasn't being realistic about my abilities any longer.

Annie was very quiet, and when she finally whined, I looked up to see the entire sky was filled with menacing-looking clouds. I'd been so caught up in my own thoughts that I hadn't paid attention to the weather, which was totally unlike me.

As a rancher, it's imperative that I know what's going on with the weather, and I listened religiously to my NOAA weather radio every day. I hadn't checked it since the day before, which made me realize how discombobulated I'd been, what with all that was going on.

I turned it on, only to find there was a severe weather warning through the evening and into tomorrow afternoon. Lightning, high winds, heavy rains, and possible hail were forecast.

As I pulled my car into the garage, I was glad I'd gone to the store. I pulled the deck furniture into the old storm cellar, then made sure all the house windows were closed. I then took Annie out for one last outing.

As I threw the ball for her, I could feel the temperature dropping, and the air had an ominous feel to it. Huge curtains of virga cloaked the distant hills, the Absaroka mountains long gone behind distant haze, which bespoke strong winds that would eventually hit the ranch, as our weather always came from that direction.

I turned and looked the other way, where huge mammatus clouds hung across the sky, black and frightening looking. I'd seen storms like this before, and one had even spawned a small tornado, which was unheard of in this part of the country. It was only mid-afternoon, yet it felt like evening.

I took Annie inside and called Lee, who said he'd already moved the haying equipment into the barn, as well as his pickup. He was expecting the worst. As I hung up, I could see the tall reeds along the irrigation ditch start to sway, and I knew the winds were coming in.

And that's when I again saw the two black figures, way out in the field, more like black dots, a small one and a big one. I got my binoculars, but they were now behind a row of trees. A chill came over me.

I really didn't want to, but I called Lee again.

"Lee, come on over for dinner."

"Thanks, Marie, but this is the night Wilson and Tom come over to play poker. Can I take a rain check?"

"Are they going to be good to drive home in this weather?" I asked, knowing full well their games of poker also involved whisky.

Lee laughed. "Probably not, but they can spend the night. They usually do, anyway—better than driving while under the weather, right?"

I laughed in spite of being disappointed. Maybe I should go spend the night at Carla's. They had a spare room, and it had been a while since I'd seen the kids.

No, something unplanned like this would just make Carla think of yet another reason I should leave the ranch. Besides, what had happened to my sense of independence and self-agency?

I fed Annie an early dinner, though it felt late. I then closed all the curtains and locked the doors, after again trying to spot the black things out in the field. There was no sight of them. The wind had started blowing in earnest, and it was sprinkling just a little.

I needed to get my mind off things. I'd do some serious cooking, make a nice lasagna and salad dinner. That would cheer me up, as well as keep me busy. I went into the kitchen, Annie at my heels.

I'd just put the lasagna into the oven when I had an overwhelming urgency to flee, to get out, to go anywhere but the house. I sat down, taking a deep breath, trying to figure out what was going on. The only other time I'd ever felt this way was the night after Bill had died. I wanted to go anywhere else, be anybody else. It was my way of trying to avoid reality, I knew.

But this felt different. It felt like raw fear, like my instincts telling me to get out, I was in danger.

I grabbed my car keys and billfold and quickly made up an overnight bag. It only took a moment, then I grabbed Annie's leash and some dog food. I was happy I'd put the car in the garage, as that way I could get into it without going outside.

I almost left the oven on, but remembered to turn it off at the last minute. I hurried Annie into the car and jumped in, then pressed the garage-door opener and backed out. It was now pouring rain, and the wind was gusting so hard it shook the car, but it wasn't completely dark, so I was able to see enough to back out the drive and head out.

As I drove away, I saw the two black figures standing right by the house. I was stunned. They *had* come back—my instincts were right! I could now see them better, and they both looked emaciated, almost starved. I felt bad for them, and they didn't look very dangerous, more like overgrown apes, though the winds had blown enough dust in that I couldn't make out any details.

I finally ended up at my friend Rowena's. She graciously put me and Annie up for the night. Like Lee, I'd known her since we were kids.

The next day, I was loathe to go home. The storm had mostly blown on through, though it was still quite windy. I figured Lee would be recovering from his poker game, so he wouldn't be any help, plus it was his day off.

I went on back to the house, where I found the front door standing wide open. I knew I'd locked it, especially since I'd been afraid of the Bigfoot or whatever they were. Lee had a key—had he come by to check on me and accidentally forgotten to lock it?

Once inside, the entire house had an odd odor. It took awhile, but I finally figured out it smelled like rotten trash. When I went into the kitchen, I found the oven door partly torn off and my lasagna gone, the empty pan on the floor. I could see where huge teeth had scraped off every last morsel of food. In addition, every cupboard was hanging open, as well as the refrigerator door, and most of my food was gone.

None of the other rooms had been touched, and nothing was stolen, so whoever it was had come for food, and they must've been really hungry to eat uncooked lasagna.

I was really shaken. My home was my safe place, my sanctuary. Would they have come inside if I'd been there? I had no idea.

I decided right then and there that I would sell out. I couldn't deal with everything anymore, especially now with these things coming inside my house, plus grizzlies starting to come around. It was all too much.

I figured that the minute I made my decision, everything would fall into place, but it didn't. Instead, I started feeling worse.

I went and lay down on my bed, confused. My shoulder had now stiffened up to where I could barely move it. And as I lay there, just feeling my emotions instead of trying to analyze everything, I knew the reason—my body was telling me I was making the wrong choice.

I called Lee, asking him to come over, even though it was his day off. He was gracious enough about it, though I knew he was suffering the effects of too much partying the night before.

"Lee," I said, "How hard would it be for you to put an electric fence around the house, a really good one that would keep a buffalo or grizzly out?"

"Are you nuts?" He asked. "You think a hotwire would keep a bear out?"

"They use them up in Canada, There's one at the Lake Louise campground, and it works just fine. I want you to build one here, a good one."

Lee shook his head. "And you think that'll keep a Bigfoot out?"

"I do," I said. "That along with the rest of my plan."

I was feeling stronger and more confident as I spoke. "I'm not selling the ranch. I'm going to lease out part of it and turn the rest into a sanctuary. But I don't want to have to worry about my house all the time. We can do this, Lee. You can stay for free in your house and live on your retirement. I can pay you an hourly wage for whatever might need doing, but it shouldn't be much, once we get it all set up. But getting this going will take some work and money."

Lee fixed the oven door while I cleaned up the kitchen, then we set to work on my new plans over a cup of coffee. I was getting more and more excited, and he was, too. We researched the type of hot wire the Canadians were using in Banff, then put in an online order for our own. We would fence the yard and a nearby acre so Annie would have lots of space to run, then fence Lee's house.

We next started drawing up landscape plans. Lee would get the old dozer and make a pond for wildlife, including for geese and waterfowl. With my water rights, I could keep it full year-round. We'd then take part of the field and plant native trees and bushes to provide wind breaks as well as places for deer and other animals to hide out.

By the time the morning was over, we were both so excited that we decided to go have lunch at the Juniper Cafe in Cody. I was feeling like a kid, this new plan having kicked something into gear I hadn't felt since Bill and I had been together. And miraculously, my shoulder had stopped hurting.

As time went on and we developed the sanctuary, I found my depression completely went away. I also started feeling better physically, my knees not as painful. I made it clear to both Carla and the real-estate woman that I had no intention of selling the ranch and was instead putting part of it into a land conservancy. The rest would be leased out, and when I was gone, Carla would inherit it and could do whatever she wanted, but the conservancy would legally be forever. To her credit, Carla now agrees I made the right choice.

I noticed that Lee also had a new spring in his step, as he was now doing something with meaning. One day, after doing some planting, he came in for a glass of iced tea.

"Marie, what we're doing here is really special. I hope you realize that."

"I hope you're right, Lee."

He replied, "You know the Bigfoot are still around, don't you?"

"I thought maybe they were, but with the hot wire up, I'm not worried about them anymore. Have you seen them?"

He laughed. "They still scare the crap out of me, you know, but I saw four of them wallowing around in the new pond just last evening. They were having a ball."

I wasn't sure what to think, so I asked, "Seen any bears?"

"No bears. I don't think they and the Bigfoot take to each other. Marie, this looks like it's turning into a Bigfoot sanctuary. Can you believe it?"

"I can't, and I don't think anyone else would, either."

"I'm going to plant a few acres of garden veggies, with your OK, of course."

"And put in a bunch of berry bushes, Lee, while you're at it. Blackberries, raspberries, whatever will grow here."

"Great idea, dear."

I smiled. "Why don't you come over for dinner?"

Lee replied, "I can't. It's my party night. How about a rain check?"

It took a couple of years, but we made that 300 acre field into a beautiful park. And you should see the critters that use it—deer, lots of waterfowl, foxes, coyotes, and even a bear or two. But our principal clients are the Bigfoot, and they seem to have taken up permanent residence, though they're secretive and only Lee has seen them, though I've seen lots of tracks. He says he sees the little one every so often, and it's filled out and looks good and is getting big.

Sometimes, we go walking out there, though we stay away from the thickets. It's a kind of paradise, and I know Bill would approve.

Oh, and I almost forget this last part—Lee kept calling me dear until I kind of got to where I liked it. He eventually moved in with me and asked me to marry him. We rented out his house to the guy who's leasing the hay fields.

We have a lot of fun, and every once in awhile he goes over to his friend's house and they drink and party, though anymore he seems to be more interested in sitting out on the front deck with his telescope.

Sometimes I ask him what he's looking for, and he just smiles and says, "You know."

8

THE MOST BEAUTIFUL PLACES

I met Jose one sunny day in the Tetons along the Buffalo Fork River, which is a tributary of the Snake. Since I was fishing in that short stretch where the Buffalo Fork flows near Moran in Grand Teton National Park, Jose's duty as a park ranger was to make sure I had a license, which of course I did.

He was a soft-spoken and personable guy, a very good representative for the Park Service. I mentioned how the Buffalo Fork was such a good wade river, and he professed he'd never been flyfishing, having grown up in arid Carlsbad, New Mexico.

It was close to his lunch break, so I gave him a short fishing lesson right then and there, then afterwards asked if he had a fishing license. We laughed about this, then got to talking about other things in our life. When I mentioned that I collect Bigfoot stories as a hobby, his face turned white, and I knew he'd had an encounter. It wasn't easy to get him to open up about it, but when he did, it was quite a story. —Rusty

. . .

My name's Jose and I live in Jackson, Wyoming, though this event took place some miles south of here, down in the northwest corner of Colorado. It's something I'll never forget, even though I wish I could.

Those who believe me (and most don't) say I'm fortunate to have seen something few get to see, but I don't really feel that way. I'm a different person than before this experience—I'm now way more cautious. And I'll also say my belief that most people are kind has faltered from the way I've been treated after telling my story. A lot of people ask to hear it, then afterwards act like I'm nuts.

Looking back later, I can say it combined the happiest and the most terrifying feelings of my life. My emotions went from one end of the spectrum to the other, all in a matter of hours.

It might make more sense if you have a little background. I'm originally from Carlsbad, New Mexico, where my parents own a pecan orchard. That area is dry and arid and, in my opinion, has very little going for it, as well as no economy, unless you want to work in the pecan orchards or the oil and gas fields.

It was an OK place to grow up, if you didn't know any better, but once I got into high school and realized that places like Yosemite and Yellowstone existed (thanks to our family vacations), all I could think of was finding a way to make a living in a beautiful place.

My mom always wanted to be a landscape painter, but how can you paint when the landscape's nothing but dry dust and wind blowing it around? I always felt kind of sad for her, though she seemed happy enough, but she did always tell me to live someplace beautiful when I grew up, as it would feed my spirit. Maybe she said that so she could come visit, which she now does quite often.

Anyway, I remember her showing me the obituary of a famous Montana landscape artist, and it said, "He always lived in the most beautiful places." I vowed then and there that I would live my life the same way, surrounded by beauty.

What does all this have to do with a Bigfoot encounter (assuming that's what it was)? Well, I was on my way to a beautiful place, a place

I intend to stay forever, when it happened. I'd been offered a job working in Grand Teton National Park. I would live in the Tetons and be surrounded by beauty.

I will say that Carlsbad's not all bad because it has Carlsbad National Park, which is a pretty incredible place. I spent a lot of time out there, and I worked summers in the cafeteria when I was in high school. One fateful day, a ranger came in and we got to talking. I think she had taken a liking to me, because she always said hello and talked to me kindly, but that particular day she started asking me about my dreams and future goals.

Well, I didn't really have any goals, but since she was a ranger, I told her I wanted to be a ranger, as it sounded good and I really liked her. She said having a college degree would be helpful. I was a senior in high school, and I had no thoughts of going to college.

I was shocked. Nobody had ever asked me about my future. Besides working the pecan orchard, my dad worked for the gas company, and my mom worked part-time in the school lunchroom, and college wasn't even on their radar. And being a park ranger? That was considered a professional job, something I never thought was in my grasp.

To make a long story short, with her encouragement, I finally got into college with student aid. I worked at Carlsbad National Park in the summers as a seasonal, doing various jobs, and went to the University of New Mexico the rest of the year, and I managed to graduate in three years with a degree in natural resources. I'd finally found what I wanted to do with my life—I would work in a national park as a ranger. Funny how one person can turn your life around.

And so, here I was, on my way to Jackson, Wyoming, going to a new job as a ranger in the Tetons, and I can easily say it was the happiest day of my life. The Tetons are a plum location—everyone wants to work there, though the winters can be brutal. I felt really fortunate to have been hired, as there were lots of applicants.

I'd checked the map carefully and knew it would be a long drive at over 1,000 miles. There was no way I could do it in one day, and since I had two weeks until the job started, I decided to take my time and do some sightseeing. Since I didn't have much money, I could camp along the way and explore as I went. It sounded exciting, an adventure, which I hadn't had much of around Carlsbad.

So, I gradually worked my way north, stopping here and there, wherever looked interesting, spending my first night at Valley of Fires Recreation Area near Carrizozo, right in the middle of extensive lava flows. It was fun and exciting, off to a new life.

Around day six, I found myself in Northwest Colorado, and I knew if I went straight north into Wyoming that the route would soon become badlands and empty stretches with nothing but sagebrush and wind. I wanted to see interesting country, so I headed for Dinosaur National Monument.

I'd read on social media about a place near there called Irish Canyon that had a small free campground in a nice setting. But the bonus was that it was a shortcut to Jackson going right across the northwestern corner of Colorado, a route that would probably take just as long, but was more interesting.

After visiting Dinosaur, I backtracked a little and stopped at the gas station in the tiny hamlet of Maybell. When I asked the attendant if the road was OK, she said it was usually in pretty good shape, though it could get washboarded.

She told me the road to Irish Canyon went near Browns Park, a lonely place, but one I should visit. Large basins were called parks by the early mountain men, and she said I should take a day to go there, as it had lots of history and interesting stuff. Butch Cassidy once hung out there, and I could visit the Gates of Lodore, where the Green River enters the deep and mysterious canyons on the edge of Dinosaur National Monument. And the Vermillion Creek drainage southeast of Irish Canyon was one of the wildest places on the planet, according to her.

As I thanked her and turned to go, she added something that seemed to be a portent.

"You be careful up there. Not long ago, they found an elk skeleton with wolf scat nearby and it had been picked clean, which is how wolves do it. Some wildlife guys came out and spotted six of them through their binoculars. We've seen them around, and it looks like a pack's made Colorado their home."

"I thought wolves pretty much left people alone," I replied. I'd read up a bunch on wolves, seeing how I would soon be a ranger in the Tetons, which has lots of wolves.

"I don't know anything about them," she replied. "But one of the wildlife guys told me there was something else with them. He found tracks. Just be careful out there by yourself."

Just as I was going to ask her more, another tourist came in and she started talking to them. I slowly went out to my car, wondering about what she'd said. There was something else with the wolves? A mountain lion? A bear? It seemed improbable and odd.

As I sat in the parking lot by the gas station studying my map, I could see that Northwest Colorado was a wild and empty landscape, and there seemed to be nothing for a good many square miles. I found it intriguing that I was close to such an empty and huge part of the West, unheard of by most people, unlike the Tetons.

I turned off the main highway and headed for Browns Park, where the road would eventually split and go to Irish Canyon. It was about a 40-mile drive, and the farther I went, the more remote it felt. I drove through a large badlands basin called Sand Wash, where I actually saw some of the wild horses that range there. That was thrilling, but also underscored how isolated it was getting.

Once in awhile, a pickup would pass going the other direction, usually some rancher type, though I didn't see many ranches. And as I got closer to Irish Canyon, I stopped seeing anyone at all, though by then it was evening and everyone was probably home.

The road finally split, one branch going to Browns Park and the other to Irish Canyon. It was late, so I decided I'd go camp, then backtrack into Browns Park the next day.

Before long, I could see a dramatic ridge rising from the sagebrush flats. The map said this was 1,000-foot high Limestone Ridge, cut in two by Irish Canyon, which I would soon find to be even more dramatic with its steep cliffs and rocks and pinyon-juniper forest.

From what I could see so far, it looked like one of those beautiful places my mom said I should surround myself with.

As I entered the canyon, I saw a sign about petroglyphs, so I stopped and followed a short trail to a square boulder with rock art on its sides and top. The sign said the rock art was made by the Fremont Indians, a culture over 1,000 years old, while more recent ones were made by Ute Indians. The figures accentuated the loneliness of the place, making me think of a lost time.

Most of the strange figures had circular eyes holding shields with various designs and spears, and there were some of bighorn sheep, but one petroglyph stood out, for it looked out of place. I went and stood near it, trying to figure it out.

It looked to be recent, for it wasn't faded and worn. I suspected it was graffiti, chiseled into the rock by someone with no regard for previous cultures. Yet it seemed serious, like it was trying to warn people, to make a statement, not to just deface the rock, yet there wasn't all that much to it. It felt kind of paradoxical.

I stood there, wondering why I sensed the maker was trying to warn people. Maybe it was because the figure they'd carved into the rock was big and bulky, like a large gorilla-type animal, something totally out of place with the surrounding canyon and other older figures. It had huge shoulders and was holding up a rock in a menacing manner, as if getting ready to throw it at whoever had made the carving.

But if that had been all, it would've just struck me as something odd, but what made it seem like a warning was its eyes and face—it had huge eyes and a face like an ape-human combination, with a flat nose and square chin and its mouth opened in a grimace. I turned away, wondering how such a primitive carving could give me a chill.

I finally reached the campground, a small site with only six spaces, all empty. Each camp spot had a picnic table and fire pit, and I was ready to pull into a site when I noticed one higher up on a small rise. I would stay up there where the star-gazing would be better, I decided.

Now, I've read stories where the person feels spooky and hesitant from the very start, but even though this campground was very isolated, I can't say I felt anything was amiss. Actually, the canyon made everything feel sheltered and secure, and I felt no sense of foreboding, as some seem to feel when in a dangerous place. It had such a nice ambience that I decided not to pitch my tent but to instead put my pad and sleeping bag on the picnic table and sleep under the stars.

I had a sandwich for dinner, not wanting to cook anything, then watched as a small flock of chukars moved through the campground. It was balmy and warm, and I knew the night would cool to the perfect temperature for sleeping, as it does in the high desert in the summers from a lack of humidity.

I watched the light play on the canyon walls, then heard what sounded like an owl, though I didn't know what kind. It sounded plaintive and far away, and as the darkness quickly enveloped everything, the canyon went from feeling welcoming to feeling lonely.

I thought about going ahead and pitching my tent, but by then it was dark and it seemed like a hassle. Besides, the stars were coming out in all their glory, and I thought of my mom and her wish for me to live in beautiful places.

I stretched out in my bag on the picnic table and thought of home, and it seemed so far away, a place I might very well never see again. Of course, I would see it many times again for holidays and such, but that night, everything seemed distant. My perfectly happy day was winding down into a night of poignancy. Had I known it would turn into fear, I would've left then and there.

I couldn't believe the stars! There was virtually no light pollution, and the stars were so thick I couldn't even make out the constellations for all the other stars. I was awestruck and felt very tiny and insignificant. After a while, it almost became too much, and I again thought about pitching my tent, but I was tired.

I would just turn over and go to sleep. I needed to get rested, for it had been a long day, and I was hoping to cut my trip short and get on up to Jackson. I was starting to miss having a hot shower and hot meals, I guess.

Just as I finally started to doze off, I heard someone way in the distance, and it sounded like they shouted, "Hey!" That's all, just a simple "Hey!" yet it seemed eerie, maybe because of the low pitch and the fact that it seemed so far away, way too far for a normal voice to carry.

I was immediately on edge. What would someone be doing way out in the middle of nowhere like this? I mean, I could understand it if they were in the campground, but it actually sounded like it came from the top of Limestone Ridge.

I decided someone must be camped up there drinking or something and had seen me come in. It was irritating, but that had to explain it, for nothing else did.

I drifted back to sleep, only to be awakened by something. I suddenly felt tense and nervous and felt for my car keys, which I'd hooked to my pants with a carabiner. Still there. What woke me? Should I get in my car?

I lay perfectly still and listened—and there it was, that same "Hey!" but now much closer. It was loud, kind of vibrating, and I wondered if someone wasn't playing games with me, using a megaphone or something. It's hard to describe, but it wasn't just loud, it had a deep tenor to it that was unnatural sounding.

How far away was it? It was hard to tell, but I knew it was no longer on the canyon rim, and it was definitely coming my way. I slipped out of my bag, ready to head for the car.

Now the hair on the back of my neck stood up, for between me and my car was a shadow—then another and another! A half-moon had now risen, and I caught a glimpse of eyes glowing in the moonlight, and from their size, I knew they were probably coyotes.

Coyotes rarely harm people, but these guys were between me and my car, and they didn't seem to be in a hurry to go away.

"Get out of here!" I said in a low voice. Coyotes are used to being hunted and will usually run off when they realize they're dealing with a human.

Instead of moving away, they seemed totally unafraid. It was then that I realized these weren't coyotes, but wolves! I thought of all the stuff I'd been reading about wolves being wary around humans, but it sure didn't seem to be true then.

I had no protection of any kind, my only advantage being that I was up higher than they were, up on the picnic table. Maybe if they tried to attack I could kick them away.

I stood up on the table, holding onto my keys for dear life, and draped the sleeping bag over my head and shoulders in an attempt to make myself look bigger. I could now see them better, as there was just enough moonlight to make out their gray coats and thick shoulders.

I tried not to be scared, as I know wild animals can sense fear pheromones, which puts you at a disadvantage, but I was terrified, and who wouldn't be?

But now the "Hey!" was closer, just behind the nearby rocks, and the wolves all turned and ran. I was stunned. Whatever was making my skin crawl was also scaring the wolves, who have no natural enemies other than one another, as they will kill other packs. Humans are their only enemy, but only when armed.

Before I could even think about it, I jumped from the table and ran to my car, keys in hand, unlocking it and jumping inside. I sat for a brief moment, trying to regain control of myself.

Did I really want to drive off and leave my clothes and expensive down sleeping bag on a picnic table? Maybe if I turned the car and shined the lights towards the table I could run and grab everything. I had extra clothes in the car, but that sleeping bag had taken half of a month's wages, as I didn't make much as a seasonal.

I hesitated, not sure what to do. I turned on my cell phone, but wasn't surprised to see I had no signal. I then rolled down my window a few inches to see if I could hear anything outside.

Everything was so quiet I was now wondering if I hadn't imagined the whole thing. Why would someone or something come down the canyon yelling "Hey!" every so often? It didn't make sense.

On impulse, without even thinking about it, I jumped out of my car and ran to the picnic table, grabbing up my stuff, then ran back.

I did it! I got everything without being attacked. Adrenaline was pumping through my veins to the point that I almost felt giddy. I actually did it!

But then, when I caught my breath, I began wondering if I'd lost my mind. There was nothing out there—it was as quiet as when I'd first come in. Should I stay and try to sleep in my car? I turned the ignition key enough to see the clock—it was 4 a.m.

Now, I heard two loud thumps, which sounded like someone whacking a nearby tree. This was odd—someone had to be here, or was it a bighorn sheep hitting it with its horns? I'd read there were bighorns in the canyon.

Now I relaxed and almost started laughing at myself. Of course it was a bighorn, and the "Hey!" sound was probably bighorns also. After all, it started way up on the canyon rim and progressed down to my camp, which a bighorn could easily and quickly traverse. I'd read about people hearing strange noises and then finding out it was some animal.

And the wolves? That could also have been curious bighorn sheep—after all, they're not very large, and their eyes would glow in the dark if there was a light source. They also have gray coats and thick shoulders.

OK, things were now starting to make sense. Should I go back to the picnic table and try to get more sleep? It was still a couple of hours until dawn. Maybe I should just make some coffee and get an early start. Or, I could catnap here in the car. Even though I now knew it was just bighorns, I still felt unsettled. I finally tried to get comfortable in the car and go back to sleep, doors locked.

I had just dozed off when I was awakened by a low growling, which turned into a deep woofing sound like a big dog would make. I finally started drifting off again to the sound of that same faraway owl.

I'd maybe slept an hour when I again woke. A loud thump had startled me from my light sleep. What was going on? Suddenly, I again heard the low growling, which went on and on, then gradually rose in tone and loudness until it ended in a high-pitched screaming.

This new event left me terrified. I knew beyond a doubt this wasn't any bighorn, nor was it a coyote or wolf. I had no idea what it could be, except maybe a mountain lion—a lion with huge lungs. And what had that thump been? It wasn't at all like the sound of someone whacking on a tree.

I could see the sky beginning to light up to the east, and I knew the long night was nearly over. I was thankful, hoping that whatever was hanging around would leave once it was daybreak.

But why wait? I was finally awake and coming to my senses. All I needed to do was start my car and head out. I could easily be in Wyoming by breakfast time. I sat up and turned the ignition key, ready to go, thinking I should've left when I'd first seen the bighorn by my picnic table. I'd be long gone, if I had.

But as I started out of the camp spot, I saw a large boulder blocking my way. I now understand what the thump noise had been. But how could it be? No human could carry something that large—it must weigh a good 500 pounds!

Someone had brought it in during the night with a backhoe, I decided, but why would they block me in? Maybe the maintenance people were getting an early start on things. Maybe they were starting some kind of construction project and didn't realize I was camped there.

In retrospect, it kind of amazes me how my mind could keep making up explanations—anything to remain in denial. Everything pointed to some kind of strange events and even possible danger, and my instincts were also verifying this, yet I kept coming up with reasons for everything, trying to make sense of it all. I guess that's how we keep from getting so scared we can't function in such situations.

Well, there I sat, unable to move forward, and no way I was getting out of my car. I would just wait until daylight, then walk down to the main road and try to get help from someone coming by.

It then occurred to me that maybe someone had come in during the night to camp, and I should go look around and catch them before they left. I was now regretting choosing the most isolated camp spot.

I was trying not to think about that scream when something hit my windshield. Rocks! Someone had just thrown a handful of gravel!

I'd been right after all. There must've been someone camped up on the rim who came all the way down to give me a hard time. They'd somehow moved that boulder into my way, and now they were throwing rocks. Only someone with hands could throw rocks, and they were also the one who'd been yelling "Hey!" at me.

What did they want? Why terrorize me? I had nothing against them. Maybe they just didn't like neighbors, but then why camp near a campground?

Crack! More rocks, but these were bigger and sounded like they'd maybe actually pitted or even cracked my windshield. I rolled my window down a little and yelled out, "Hey! Knock it off!" I knew this probably would just egg them on, and I felt stupid afterwards for doing it.

As I anticipated, this just brought down a bigger barrage. I was now seriously feeling threatened. What if they meant to kill me? I honked my horn and yelled, "I have a gun," which of course I didn't.

Again, I immediately felt stupid, knowing no one would believe me. I was just antagonizing them, and they were probably enjoying my distress.

Now more rocks, but these were even larger. One came down on my hood, leaving a good dent. I was now debating whether or not to get out and run, for if a big enough rock came through the windshield, it could seriously injure me, or worse. Another bounced off the roof, landing close enough that I could tell it was a good foot in diameter.

I then realized it was dawn, for I could now see what was being lobbed at me. And yet, there was no sign of whoever was doing the lobbing. Another scream let me know they were still there and just as angry.

There was something so primal about that scream, so utterly terrifying that it seemed to take me back to a time when humans lived in a constant state of danger, with no shelter and only meagre weapons like spears for protection.

Life must've always been on the edge for those living such primitive lives, just like that dawn in Irish Canyon was for me. But one major difference between these early people and me was that they expected danger, it was always there, whereas I'd gone to sleep peacefully star gazing and had awakened to something so far from my experience I didn't even know how to categorize it.

As I waited for another round of rocks, shaking and unsure of what to do, I thought back to the petroglyph I'd seen on the rocks at the canyon's mouth. It hadn't seemed very old at all, and now I suspected it had to be recent. Someone else had gone through what I was and had made the drawing to warn others. The problem was, it didn't make sense until it was too late and you were already experiencing it.

Crash! Another rock landing on the hood. It looked like it had caved it in a good six inches, if not more.

I again rolled my window down a little, then started yelling. "Go away! I haven't done anything to you. Please go away!"

I couldn't help but start sobbing uncontrollably. For some reason, I could see my mom's face and hear her saying, "Jose, beautiful places will feed your soul, your spirit." Had her influence brought me here? If I hadn't wanted to work in national parks, I'd probably still be working in the pecan orchard in the summers and working in the Carlsbad cafeteria the rest of the year.

Who knows, I might've been happy living the quiet life, just as my parents did. I wouldn't be preparing to die here in Irish Canyon at the ripe old age of 22.

Some people enjoy the comfort of stability, living life the same way day after day, but I knew I wasn't one of them. If I'd stayed in Carlsbad, I knew I'd be unhappy with no obvious way to better myself.

So, even if I died here at the hand of some strange person or creature I had yet to even see, I knew I was living the kind of life I needed to live. Ironic, I thought, thinking you were living the good life while you might be dying.

My sobbing soon wore itself out, and just then, I caught a glimpse of my adversary—just a glimpse, but enough to know it was not human. It was a huge black figure with its hand open as if ready to throw something, its hair having a reddish-brown tinge and hanging down from its arms a good six inches.

And just like that, it was gone into the shadowy trees. I watched, waiting for it to come back, maybe with some large rock it had gone to fetch, but I knew it was gone when I heard that scream again, only from a good quarter mile away.

Had it really left, or was there a second one? I could now hear the sound of an engine down in the campground. I tried to open my car door, but it was jammed shut from the impact of all the rocks, the frame probably bent. I scooted to the other door, but couldn't get it open either.

I panicked. Whoever was down there was my only hope! I began honking the horn over and over and yelling at the top of my lungs. It seemed like it took forever, but soon an old Ford pickup drove up and two guys got out. They looked to be some of the rancher types I'd surmised used the road.

I rolled my window down all the way and told them my door was stuck. They looked shocked, and one asked, "What happened here?"

I didn't know them from Adam, and all I wanted was to be rescued, so I downplayed it by saying there'd been a rockslide, even though I wasn't close to the canyon wall.

"Why not climb out the window?" One of the guys asked, making me feel like a fool. But I didn't care, I was just glad to see them. I crawled out, and we introduced ourselves. Their names were Jerry and Jim, and they walked around, examining my car, which now looked inoperable, the hood smashed down onto the engine.

Jerry asked, "How did this big rock get there on the road?"

"I don't know," I replied. "It all happened during the night."

After surveying the situation, they got a tow strap from their truck and managed to wrap it around the rock and drag it off to the side of the road. They then hooked their pickup to my car, which miraculously enough, was still able to move, and they towed me back to

Maybell, which seemed to take forever on that dusty dirt road. But I didn't mind, I was just happy to be out of that place.

They wouldn't let me pay them, but they did let me buy them breakfast at the little restaurant there. I called roadside service, and they eventually came and towed my car to the town of Vernal, Utah, where the body shop said it wasn't worth repairing.

I ended up buying a cheap car in Vernal, thanks to my dad sending me the cash. I barely made it to Jackson in time to start my job, and I will say it took me another month or two to start feeling like my old self again, though the other park employees didn't notice, as they hadn't been around me before. They probably thought I was naturally quiet and subdued.

I'd taken a photo of my bashed-up car, and I carried it around in my pocket for some time, just to remind myself it had really happened and wasn't a dream.

I've since been half-afraid to go out on the trails in Grand Teton National Park alone, though the park encourages us to go in pairs in the deeper wilderness, because of the bears. But I'm gradually getting over everything, though sometimes I still have nightmares about hearing rocks thudding nearby.

But what I'm still trying to process is what Jerry and his friend Jim told me over breakfast.

"We know what happened, and you're not the first," Jim told me over a cup of coffee. "We call it the Irish Fuddler, 'cause that's how it leaves your brain, befuddled. As far as we know, it's actually never harmed anyone."

"Some folks have a lot stronger name for it than that," Jerry added. "It left plenty of tracks at your camp, right by the wolf ones. But your car is the worst we've seen so far. This thing came into this country just a year or so ago, and there's been talk about trying to hunt it down. If it keeps this kind of stuff up, it'll have a posse out looking for it."

"Where did it come from?" I asked.

"Nobody knows," Jerry said. "But a few reports have come out of the Yampa Canyon area, which is pretty wild country. The only people ever in there are rafters. We're hoping it'll move on out, go somewhere away from people."

"Have you seen it?" I asked.

Jim replied, "I saw it crossing the road up there by Irish Canyon late one night. Caught a glimpse of it in my headlights. It scared the bejeebers out of me. Jerry and I have a contract with the Bureau of Land Management to keep up the campground, that's why we happened to be there this morning. We only go in once a week to pick up trash and that kind of thing. We never come in here alone anymore. You were lucky it was our day to be there."

"I guess," I said, though I didn't feel very lucky, thinking about the strange petroglyph that looked just like the creature I'd seen.

Jim added, "We had a couple of climbers come in and camp at the beginning of the summer. They had a pretty scary experience and took it upon themselves to carve a picture there with the petroglyphs. We couldn't prove they did it, but the BLM was pretty upset about that. They're planning on eventually restoring it."

"I saw that," I replied. "I wish I'd known what it stood for. I would've kept on going."

Jerry laughed. "Maybe we should put up a Bigfoot warning sign."

"Might be a good idea," I said lamely, then thanked them again and bid them farewell, knowing I'd never be back.

9

THE BIG WINDS BLOWDOWN

Scottie and Claudia own an outdoors store in a tourist town not far from where I live, and when I was in there one day looking for a good waterproof jacket, we got to talking about camping and hiking. Of course, it's a topic they know a lot about, given what they do for a living.

After getting me outfitted in a nice jacket and even giving me a discount, I happened to mention I was heading for Montana. They asked if I took the route from Colorado up through Pinedale, Wyoming. I said I did if Yellowstone was open, as it was the most direct way. We then started talking about the beautiful Wind River Range, which that drive parallels. They then told me the following story. —Rusty

Rusty, it's funny how your mind can create associations that stick with you long after an event, and that's how I am now with the smell of wet dogs. To this day, if I smell a wet dog, my initial response is a sense of panic. I am getting better with time, and I really do love dogs, but I have to be careful if I'm around them.

What would cause such an odd thing? I mean, you have an anxiety attack when you smell a wet dog? I don't tell many people about it, that's for sure. But it was caused by association with a traumatic event. It seems our minds go into overdrive during trauma, analyzing everything around us, some of it on a subconscious level. I don't even remember smelling wet dogs during what happened, but my husband Scottie does—he says it was an overpowering stench. It's funny, because it didn't have that effect on him at all, and wet dogs don't bother him, unless they get him wet or something, but instead he gets anxious when the wind picks up. So the same things can really affect us differently.

My name's Claudia, and since all this happened so recently, I'm hoping the memory will fade with time. It's not everyday that you get to not only almost die in a horrible windstorm but are also visited by creatures you thought were a myth.

But that's about par for the Wind River Range in Wyoming, a place long associated with legends of all kinds—some told by the Northern Shoshone and Northern Arapaho, whose combined reservation is on the east side of the range.

The Winds contain over 1,300 named lakes, seven of the 10 largest glaciers in the lower 48, and more than 40 peaks over 13,000 feet. They're like a dreamland with rugged granite spires and walls that provide an epic backdrop to world class backpacking, fishing, horsepacking, and climbing. Once you've been there, you fall in love with it, and it's like the old saying, when you give yourself to places, they give you yourself back.

Most of the backpackers come in on the west side of the Winds near the town of Pinedale, and that's where Scottie and I started on a trip we'd planned for over a year. Our route was the popular trail from Elkhart Park to Titcomb Basin, which goes to Photographer's Point above Fremont Lake and ends deep in the heart of the Winds.

It was early September, one of the best times to be in the Wind Rivers, as the mosquitoes are almost gone and the fall colors are starting. The Winds are famous for their mosquitoes, which have run many a hiker out, and the black flies can be just as vicious.

We started out on Labor Day weekend, a beautiful day with blue skies and golden aspens. We'd checked the weather, but hadn't seen anything threatening. We live in Colorado and had driven up the night before.

Things can change quickly in the mountains, as we found out, though being from Colorado, we pretty much already knew this. We've seen our share of unexpected storms and have been hunkered down more than once in unpredicted snowstorms, though most usually sweep over and are soon gone.

But that weekend was one for the books. Actually, let me quote from a Forest Service bulletin that was put out shortly after the storm:

> The mountains have experienced a massive storm over the Labor Day weekend. Many trails are most likely closed or nearly impassable due to huge timber blowdowns extending for miles. Reports are coming from Search and Rescue, the Bridger-Teton National Forest, and others of harrowing stories, terrible conditions, and blocked and timber-clogged trails. Many of the stories involve backcountry users who were not prepared for conditions.

This massive storm and wind event rolled through the Wind Rivers on Monday, four days after we'd headed into the backcountry. The 80 m.p.h. winds that followed the storm downed thousands of trees, some in stacks up to 10 feet deep. Most of the roads and trails into the Winds became impassable within hours, and the trail we'd hiked from Photographer's Point was completely erased in places as if an avalanche had swept through.

OK, we started in on a Friday and the storm hit on Monday. What about those three days before it hit? Well, like I mentioned, Friday was an awesome day, nice and clear and beautiful. We spent some time at Photographer's Point taking photos, getting ourselves psyched up for carrying our heavy packs into the high country.

Photographer's Point has a beautiful little tarn, or glacial lake, that's situated where you can get a nice shot of the Winds in the background. Sometimes I look at my photos and am still shocked at how quickly a place can change in just a matter of a few hours. Some of the beautiful evergreens that are nicely reflected in the tarn in my photos are now just stumps and debris.

Keep in mind that the storm didn't just blow down dead trees, but took out healthy ones, too, pulling them up by their root balls. Some of these trees were three feet in diameter.

Anyway, we made it to Seneca Lake for our first camp Friday night. It was an incredible night sky with thousands of stars reflecting in the still lake and the Milky Way arcing above. I had a hard time making myself go to bed, even though Scottie was already asleep.

If you've ever been to Seneca Lake, you'll know that, like most of the terrain in the Winds, it's surrounded by granite terrain that's been rounded by glaciation until it looks like hummocks. Above all that are huge granite cliffs, many of which have been sculpted into incredible spires and watchtowers. Because the terrain is so rugged, hiking in the Winds can be very challenging.

As I sat there, looking into the deepest night sky imaginable, I felt a sense of fragility. Even though Scottie was nearby in the tent, I felt like I was totally alone in the entire universe. I think the immensity and rawness of the place made me aware of my mortality and insignificance.

I shivered even though it wasn't all that cold, maybe around 45 degrees, a typical early autumn night in the mountains. Soon, coming from far away, I heard a *thunk thunk*, as if someone was hitting a tree with a branch. It was so far away I had to strain to make it out, but there it was again!

I suddenly felt nervous, even though it was far away, and I knew it had to be other campers. Even at that, it felt odd and creepy, so I called it a night and crawled into the tent and promptly fell asleep.

We were up early the next morning, which was Saturday. Even though we'd gotten an early start, coming in Friday, we still expected to see other people, but it was as quiet as could be. What we didn't know was that the weather forecast had changed, resulting in most hikers bailing.

We spent the day hiking to Island Lake, which put us within striking distance of Titcomb Basin. We would dayhike to the basin on

Sunday, then return to our camp at Island Lake Sunday night, then head back down, spending Monday night at Hobbs Lake and returning to the trailhead on Tuesday. Of course, we had no idea that the weather had other plans in store for us.

Island Lake is a beautiful lake with several islands, as one might guess by its name. A lot of people like to hike into the Winds to fish, especially for the elusive golden trout, but Scottie and I were content to do nothing, just eat sandwiches and enjoy the evening view. We were both happy there were only a handful of mosquitoes, which made us believe the Winds had had at least one good frost before we arrived.

Finally, not long before sunset, we saw a pair coming our way up the trail from the lake. As they got closer, we could tell they were rangers, and they stopped to inform us our camp was too close to the lake and we would need to move.

Since it was almost dark, they helped us pick everything up, showing us a spot near their own camp, which we hadn't noticed on the way in as it was above us. We knew that camping close to the lakes was prohibited for environmental reasons, but we'd underestimated our distance.

Once our camp was reestablished, we invited the two rangers to have some hot chocolate with us. Both guys were really knowledgeable, and we learned a lot about the mountains and their residents, which did include grizzlies, though not many.

I finally asked if they'd been chopping wood the previous night, but they said no. When I explained why I'd asked, one looked mildly irritated while the other explained that it was probably just nearby campers.

I later asked Scottie why that would irritate the guy, and he laughed, saying maybe it was a Bigfoot and since the rangers are trained to not alarm the public, the guy didn't want to go there.

I knew Scottie was kidding, but it made me nervous anyway. I'd never given Bigfoot much thought at all, and this wasn't the place I wanted to start, way out here in the wilderness.

I didn't sleep well that night, and I thought it was from thinking about things that go bump in the night, but later I wondered if it wasn't from the incoming storm. It didn't help matters much when just before dawn a small bird started singing by our tent and continued until we left. I took a photo of it and later identified it as a white-crowned sparrow. Once again, I later wondered if it didn't have something to do with the storm, but at the time I was irritated.

That morning seemed sullen and even quieter than before with nobody around. It was Sunday, and the storm would hit the next day, though we weren't aware of that fact.

We weren't close enough to the rangers' camp to know if they'd left or not. We hastily made up a lunch and grabbed our daypacks and headed for Titcomb Basin, which would be a nine-mile roundtrip to the north shore of Upper Titcomb Lake.

As we made our way up the trail, I pointed out a perfect lenticular cloud above us shaped like a cigar. High above that was another, though this one was shelf-shaped and extended as far as we could see. Lenticulars come from winds high above. Was a storm coming in?

Titcomb Basin exceeded our expectations, reminding me a little of the famous Cirque of the Towers further south with its similar huge granite spires. I was again curious as to why no one was there, but got lots of nice people-free photos. On our way back, we had to stop and take photos at the waterfall that feeds from the Titcomb Basin lakes into Island Lake.

As we sat there, ready to head back, Scottie commented that we not only hadn't seen any people, but we also hadn't seen any wildlife at all on this trip, not even a moose, though they're usually in the lower meadows. We always see moose.

We hadn't even seen a marmot, and they're everywhere, waiting to steal food when you're not looking. No pikas, no ground squirrels, nothing. And come to think of it, the only bird we'd seen the entire trip was that little sparrow that had woken us up that morning.

We now hurried back, realizing that our sidetrack to the waterfall had cost us more time than we wanted. We'd planned to spend that night again at Island Lake, but we were now wondering if we couldn't make it back down to Seneca Lake if we really hurried. If we spent the night there, we could skip Monday night at Hobbs Lake and get a room in Pinedale instead and spend an extra day there.

Now let me say that we've never cancelled a trip early. If anything, we have to persuade each other to go out when we're supposed to so as to not risk losing our jobs. So for us both to be feeling like we wanted to cut the trip short was very unusual, and those lenticulars didn't help.

As we approached our camp, we heard someone yelling, and the two rangers soon hurried over. They were waiting to tell us the weather forecast had changed for the worse. They had a satellite phone and had received an urgent message and needed to get going to warn anyone on the trail. They were leaving immediately and told us we should, too. The incoming storm had been seriously upgraded.

Anyone who backpacks into the Winds after September should be prepared for some snow and cold temperatures, and we were, but there was no way we were prepared for what the new forecast said was coming. It called for several feet of snow in the higher basins, but what was scary was the forecast for high winds.

The higher the altitude, the higher the winds, and the forecast called for 60 to 80 m.p.h. in the valleys. We found out later that the town of Green River, Wyoming had 80 m.p.h. winds that did millions in damage. It was easy to deduct that the mountains would see much higher winds.

It was a no-brainer decision to head out, and we quickly packed our tent and gear. We were hoping the rangers would wait up for us, but they had a mission and were already long gone.

By then, it was afternoon and we'd already hiked a good nine miles into Titcomb Basin, so we were tired. But we felt panicked, which gave us new energy. I kept out some energy bars and handed a couple to Scottie to eat on the way. We hurried as fast as we could, trying to make good time while we still had light.

I knew Scottie was worried, as he pretty much set a pace of half-running, dodging his way down the trail, bouncing off rocks. I was worried one of us would sprain an ankle, so I pretty much had to force him to slow down by taking the lead. He wasn't happy about slowing down, but he conceded I was right—a twisted ankle could mean disaster at this point.

Now a breeze had picked up, nothing to normally worry about, except we knew it was a precursor to what was coming. 80 m.p.h. or higher winds? How could we even survive that?

As twilight fell, we pulled out our headlamps and continued on, but it wasn't long before we couldn't make anything out in terms of a trail. It's not like trails in the Wind Rivers are all that defined anyway—sometimes they consist of nothing but rock cairns, which are impossible to find in the dark. What is obvious in daylight becomes a guessing game after dark.

We finally had no choice but to stop. We found a small depression and put up our tent, the wind now picking up enough to whip it around as we tried to pitch it. I tried to hide how I felt from Scottie, but I was quickly becoming truly scared.

We took special care to securely pound in our tent stakes and then kept as much gear in our packs as possible, just in case we had to flee. Normally, we'll put our packs in our tent vestibule, but we brought them inside, thinking the extra weight would help keep us from sailing away.

We next slipped into our warm winter clothes—wool long johns and sweaters and socks, and lay our hats, gloves, and waterproof coats out, ready to put on, for we knew we'd be hiking out in snow in the morning. We then made a good hot dinner of freeze-dried spaghetti, followed by hot tea.

By then, the winds had really picked up. We had no idea how far we were from Seneca Lake, but we'd made good time, so it was maybe only a mile or so away—but then there were all the miles back to Photographers Point and eventually the car. I had a sinking feeling we were doomed.

We both lay in our sleeping bags, feeling the temperature drop by the minute. Finally, the winds began to seriously pick up, and we could hear hail begin to fall on the tent. Scottie looked out the vestibule to see it was pea-sized, which quickly turned to marble-sized.

We hadn't counted on hail, which can quickly shred your tent. Combined with wind, a tent can turn into a bunch of nylon strips in mere minutes. Scottie crawled back into his bag and we lay there, lost in our own fears and thoughts.

It wasn't long before the winds were howling, gusts smacking the tent into our faces and slapping the vestibule. I tried to say something to Scottie, but the wind was so loud he couldn't hear me. He reached over and took my hand, and we lay there holding each other's hands, trying to sleep, which was basically impossible.

Well, not totally impossible, because I woke with a start, which meant I had to have been sleeping, as we were both exhausted. At this point, the wind was deafening, except for the trees I could hear falling, some nearby, some a little farther away. And now lightning was popping overhead and all around us, lighting up the interior of the tent to where I could see Scottie with his bag pulled up over his head.

I tried to recall if we'd pitched our tent anywhere close to a tree, but since it had been dark, I wasn't sure. I had accepted that we would probably die out there, so it seemed like a moot point anyway. Crack! Another tree down, then another, and another.

I read later that so many trees were downed that several horseback camps had to be rescued by people with chainsaws cutting their way out, as it was an impossible passage otherwise. An outfitter out of Pinedale said that nine of his 11 hunting tents were crushed by trees and the other two shredded.

Now a huge gust slammed against us and I could feel the tent actually start to scoot along a few inches, stakes popping out, with us in it. The tent poles were so bowed that there was barely room above our faces to breathe, and I knew it was only a matter of time before the poles snapped.

But suddenly, even though I could still hear the wind screaming, the tent had now popped back up, as if the wind had stopped. How could the winds have stopped when I could still hear them howling like a banshee?

I then realized that something was serving as a windbreak, and it had to be something fairly large. Had a rock rolled down next to the tent? If so, we were really lucky to not have died.

Just then, the winds were back. A big gust hit, catching the tent and snapping the main pole with a crack, everything collapsing around us, the wind biting through a hole ripped in the nylon by the pole.

It was then that the tent began moving upward until we were suspended in the air, all tumbled on top of each other with our gear. It was as if two people had picked the entire tent up from either end with us in it and were now carrying us along. It felt like being in the saddlebags of a moving horse.

I knew it had to be an illusion and that we were being swept off the mountain by the winds. It was a feeling of incredible helplessness, as well as being very uncomfortable, all packed together, me on top of Scottie and our packs on top of me. Fortunately, I'm a small person, and I just hoped he could breathe.

This went on for some time, being carried along like helpless rag dolls, all the while surrounded by the sound of trees cracking like matchsticks. I finally realized that we were being carried along by something other than the wind, though I had no idea what it could be.

And through the sound of the howling wind, I could hear the deep guttural grunting of whoever was carrying us, a sound like I've never heard before. It chilled me even more than the wind, making me wonder if we weren't being carried to our destiny, a fate we wouldn't wish on our enemies.

Suddenly, the tent was carefully lowered back down. I rolled off Scottie, and we managed to push our packs to the side. Everything was upside down, the tent's zipper now beneath us, and I started feeling the panic of claustrophobia. What was going on? I could still hear the wind, but it was now distant, as if we were in some kind of room.

Now the stench of wet dogs enveloped everything. It had probably been with us all along, as I later figured out we'd been carried by two large smelly creatures, but the wind had mitigated it. But now it was so strong I could barely breathe, and it made me want to throw up.

Scottie and I both lay there very still, afraid to move. We could now hear heavy breathing, as well as more guttural sounds, but whoever it was, they were being quiet. The wind was still howling, but no longer blowing us around. I wanted badly to open the tent's zipper to see who was there but couldn't reach it, which was probably a good thing. We both eventually fell asleep.

We talked about this endlessly afterwards, trying to find some closure and decided we were rescued by two Bigfoot, as crazy as that sounds. We never did see them, but what else could carry two people and their gear like that? They'd somehow come upon us and carried us over to their own sheltering place, then left after the winds had blown on through.

When daylight finally came, we managed to get out of the tent and could see we were in a small natural shelter that had been formed by several huge rocks leaning against each other, probably pushed together thousands of years ago by glaciers. There was no one else there. We managed to find our way out of the tent, which was damaged beyond repair.

Looking out, we could see it was snowing, but the winds had passed. We collected our gear, leaving the tent, and began making our way out. We were lost at first, but our GPS helped us find our way to Seneca Lake, then on down to Hobbs Lake and eventually to Photographer's Point and the parking area.

I make this sound like a cakewalk, and even though it was snowing, the snow wasn't a problem, as it had only snowed a few inches by then—the problem was the trees. They covered the trail to the point it was totally gone, and at times it seemed like we would never find a way forward. We climbed over and under trees, all the time aware that more could come down on us.

It's hard to put into words the condition of the mountains after the storm, the mass of tangled trees—it truly looked like a war zone. It took us two days to get out, and fortunately the snow was light that first day. We were able to make a shelter under some fallen trees that first night and stay warm, even without our tent. We awoke the next morning to about 20 inches of snow, and it was still coming down.

Once we finally got back to Pinedale, we had to stay an extra night because all the highways to Colorado were closed. While there, we went to a local bar that had become a gathering place, and we heard many stories. The aftermath of the storm presented many challenges for the search and rescue team there, and rescue plans changed hourly as more information was gathered about the damage and those missing. Many hikers left the mountains upon hearing the forecast and got out safely, but those like us who got the message too late experienced a storm like none other.

One group of five hikers had requested emergency pickups with their satellite beacons because the storm had destroyed their tents and scattered their belongings all over the mountains. Another group sent an SOS, having lost their way.

There were lots of stories, and yet no one was even seriously injured, even though there were a few helicopter rescues. The majority of people that were in the woods were OK, other than being bruised and scared.

Scottie and I finally got back home, where I swear it took us two weeks to recover. I think most of that was more mental than physical, though spending two days crawling around and over trees had been exhausting.

In spite of all our discussion and trying to figure it out, we're still puzzled by what happened. Were we really rescued by Bigfoot? Was it a shared hallucination of some kind? If it was real, what would've happened to us if they hadn't come along? We were still pretty high up, and who knows where we would've landed in hurricane-force winds?

It's all very surreal feeling, but whatever happened, we feel very fortunate to have survived the big blowdown in the Winds that September. When we get the courage up to go back in, we're going to retrieve our destroyed tent, partly because we follow the leave no trace ethic, but partly because we want to see that shelter again.

I know it will be an eerie feeling if we can find it, though Scottie has the GPS coordinates. Knowing that Bigfoot use it might make me kind of hesitant to go back, but again, knowing they saved us, I want to leave some kind of tribute or gift for them. I'm not sure what that would be, but maybe a big box of beef jerky.

ABOUT THE AUTHOR

Rusty Wilson is a fly-fishing guide based in Colorado and Montana. He's well-known for his Dutch-oven cookouts and campfires, where he's heard some pretty wild stories about the creatures in the woods, especially Bigfoot.

Whether you're a Bigfoot believer or not, we hope you enjoyed this book, and we know you'll enjoy Rusty's many others, the first of which is *Rusty Wilson's Bigfoot Campfire Stories*. Also check out Rusty's bestselling *Montana Bigfoot Campfire Stories* and *Yellowstone Bigfoot Campfire Stories,* as well as *Bigfoot: The Dark Side, The Creature of Lituya Bay,* and *Chasing After Bigfoot: My Search for North America's Most Elusive Creature.*

Rusty's books come in ebook format, as well as in print and audio.

You'll also enjoy the first book in the Bud Shumway mystery series, a Bigfoot mystery, *The Ghost Rock Cafe.*

Other offerings from Yellow Cat Publishing include an RV series by RV expert Sunny Skye, which includes *Living the Simple RV Life.* And don't forget to check out the books by Sunny's friend, Bob Davidson: *On the Road with Joe,* and *Any Road, USA.* And finally, you'll love Roger Dean Miller's comedy thriller, *Bombing Hoffman.*

Made in the USA
Las Vegas, NV
24 November 2023